CARTEL PUBLICATIONS
PRESENTS

THE ORIGINAL
CLASSIC

Black and Ugly

T. STYLES

NATIONAL BEST-SELLING AUTHOR OF *RAUNCHY*

ARE YOU ON OUR EMAIL LIST?

SIGN UP ON OUR WEBSITE

www.thecartelpublications.com

OR TEXT THE WORD: CARTELBOOKS

TO 22828

FOR PRIZES, CONTESTS, ETC.

4   *Black and Ugly*

By T. Styles

A School of Dolls

Kali: Raunchy Relived The Miller Family

The End. How To Write A Bestselling Novel in 30 Days

WWW.THECARTELPUBLICATIONS.COM

Black and Ugly

Black and Ugly

BY

T. STYLES

(Originally Published in 2007)

PUBLISHER'S NOTE:
This book is a work of fiction. Names, characters,
businesses,
Organizations, places, events and incidents are the
product of the
Author's imagination or are used fictionally. Any
resemblance of
Actual persons, living or dead, events, or locales are
entirely coincidental.

Library of Congress Control Number: 2006937037
ISBN 10: 0996209956
ISBN 13: 978-0996209953
Cover Design: Davida Baldwin www.oddballdsgn.com
www.thecartelpublications.com
First Edition
Printed in the United States of America

DEDICATION

I'd like to dedicate this novel to all my chocolate sisters who don't realize how truly beautiful you are.

#BlackAndUgly

CHAPTER 1

PARADE KNIGHT

I knew I was ugly the moment my mother gave me a mirror. How could I not? Growing up, she reminded me over and over that I didn't look like her when she was younger. I don't care too much, anymore, because I can beat a bitch down. And, I dare somebody to call me ugly to my face. Everybody knows me 'round my way and, they know, the one thing I don't tolerate is someone telling me something I already know.

Hyattsville, Maryland, where I was born and raised, is not always considered the ghetto until you lift up a few rocks and look behind a couple of corners. Then, you'll come face to face with what moves in the dark because, in the most remote part of town, and next to a cemetery, is Quincy Manor apartments, the place I've called my home for 22 years ...and that's all my life.

By the way, I'm Parade Knight. I'm 5'5", dark-skin and thick to death. I'm the one the boys sneak around with when their girlfriends act up...well... besides Miss Wayne, and that's a whole 'notha story. I'm not light-skin or pretty enough to be their arm-piece, but I'm soft enough to put in their beds. I've been told that I don't give them a hard time like their girls do, that's why they fucks with me.

Although I know I'm not the prettiest, my body is tight and my pussy stays wet. I've learned to appreciate my positives and ignore the negatives. Does it hurt to be considered unattractive? Yeah, it does. But I've gotten use to it over time. There's no use in me dwelling on shit I can't change. I'm gonna be ugly today, and I'm gonna be ugly tomorrow. Might as well make the best of what God gave me. Right?

Now my friends, they're just the opposite of me. Take Sky Taylor for instance. We're the same height, age and weight, about 145 pounds but her hair is soft, short and naturally curly. Her skin is light and she ain't got a mark on her body. Get a good picture of her in your head. Can you see her? Well, I'm the exact opposite.

Sky gives me a lot of things, like the clothes she doesn't want anymore. I wish we had the same shoe size because she buys a new pair every week. I don't care if they're hand-me-downs, 'cuz without her, I wouldn't have anything decent to wear. She even gave me this fly ass perfume that my mother stays coming in my room using. And that doesn't do anything but piss me off because when it's gone, she ain't got no intention on replacing it.

My folks give me the bare essentials. A comb. A brush. Soap. Food. A roof over my head. If my shoes wear out and began to speak, maybe…just maybe, they'll buy me a new pair. Other than that, I'm short dog. Now my, so-called, man gives me a few dollars every now and again, but not enough to buy no real clothes.

I often ask myself, "If Sky looks out for you, why do you fuck her man?" My answer to that is this: the outfits, the perfume and Jay bring me closer to actually being her…until he calls me an ugly black bitch, or I look into the mirror.

I am just sitting, on my black canopy bed, wondering what I'm gonna get into on a Thursday night and my phone rings. I'm hoping it ain't my boyfriend 'cuz, sometimes, I'd rather be alone than with him. He grosses me out. It's just a matter of time before I end things but, first, I have to make sure it's what I wanna do. I guess, if I hadn't been fucking Sky's man for the past six months, I wouldn't know what a real man's touch feels like, but now I do. So, I don't want to replace that so quickly for Melvin's short, stubby fingers.

"Hello," I answered the phone.

"What the deal, Parade? Your folks up? 'Cuz I was trying to slide through there and bang the walls out of that pussy right quick," he says.

It's him. Jay! He's been calling me a lot lately. At first, he would sneak over here once a week but, now, he's over here every other day.

"They ain't even here," I respond, hoping my smile doesn't come through the phone. "I thought you were taking Sky to the movies in 40 minutes."

"I am," he answers, breathing heavily as if he's irritated. "How you know?"

"She called me and said she was on her way to meet you down there. If you come see me, and we do what we do, you won't have time to shower."

"It ain't like we don't live in the same complex, Parade," he says. "Anyway are you worried about it?"

He knows I ain't worried. I have splotches, acne and bumps all over my face. There is no way on earth I am turning down Jay Hernandez, who if dressed like a girl, still looks better than me. At 6'3", 230 pounds, he is handsome, fit, strong and the only man other than 5'4" Melvin who wants to be bothered with me.

"No…it's just that…you know how Sky is when she gets around you. She'll probably want to go down on you or something in the movie theater, and then what?"

Black and Ugly

"And then I'll let her do it," he says, aggravated at my question. "Man, stop asking me so much 'cuz I ain't feeling the third degree. That's the same kinda shit I can't stand about her ass."

"I'm not trying to get you mad," I respond as I sit up in the bed and play with the hole in the multicolored comforter. "It's just that...well, I feel bad when you see me right before you see her."

"Look...we do what we do but, if you ain't feeling it...fuck it. I won't come over," he says and hangs up.

I stand up. My heart is racing, and I'm already feeling as if I've lost a boyfriend instead of a slide, somebody I fuck from time to time. What am I gonna do now? Asking a million questions had ruined my chances of being with Jay tonight. And what if he never wants to see me again? I'm so fucking stupid. Why would I remind him about his girlfriend when he is coming over my house to see me?

I walk into the kitchen to get something to eat. But, in my heart, I'm trying to get my mind off needing to feel him and hold him. I grab a plate and a piece of five-day-old fried chicken out the fridge. I'm trying to get my mind off Jay but the red phone shining on the kitchen wall stands out to me. I take it as a sign. Maybe I should call him, and at least tell him I'm sorry. After all, it is my fault for asking so many stupid-ass questions. What he does with Sky is none of my business, and I have no right questioning him. I'll call and if he still doesn't want to see me...well, at least I know I apologized.

I pick up the phone and nervously dial his number. Please let him still be available.

"Yeah," he yells as the sounds of Biggie's "Fuck You Tonight" blasted on his truck stereo in the background.

"Jay...it's Parade," I say as my voice begins to shake. "Can you turn your music down a little?"

He does but remains silent.

"Uh...I wasn't trying to get you mad," I continue, twirling the phone cord and playing with the fried chicken I have no intention of eating.

Silence.

"I will never question you again. I understand what you guys do ain't got shit to do with me."

Silence.

"And if you still wanna come by...I still wanna see you."

Sweat forms on my head and I raise my left brow as I wait for his response. Am I tripping off him more than I realize? Is my heart getting too deep into a man who at any point could say, game over. I don't feel like playing anymore. Where would that leave me? Back with sweaty-ass Melvin? I hope not.

"Leave the door open, and don't have shit on," he demands.

I hurry into the bathroom to freshen up. I put on the BeBe perfume Sky gave me, take a rat-tail comb then smooth some gel on the back of my hair so it will stay in place. My mother never taught me how to style it when I was in high school. Instead, she use to cut it all off so she didn't have to deal with it so, now, I keep it slicked down real low with a part on the side. I usually cut it myself with a pair of scissors.

Whenever Jay comes over, I want to look nice for him. Part of me hopes he'd think about me when he leaves. Don't think I'm wrong, and don't make your mind up about me yet. I care about Sky, but I also know she talks bad about me when I'm not around. Whenever something's wrong with her, she takes it out on me. She don't do the same thing to Miss Wayne or Daffany, and we've all been best friends forever.

Between her and my mother, I don't know who comes down on me the worst.

Even though Sky wails on me, I'll fuck somebody up about her. I got a reputation for fighting and stomping bitches out 'round the way. That's the only reason they don't fuck with me. Most of the scratches, on my face, came from beating a bitch's ass.

So it's not like I'm fucking Sky's man and don't care about her. It's just that...I need Jay to make me

By T. Styles   17

feel like a woman and, sometimes, even pretty. Hell, she can get anybody she wants, but I can't. So what am I supposed to do?

He's here. Damn! It's only been five minutes. He walks straight through the door because it's already open. Ooooohh, he's looking soooo good. Have you ever seen a man who looked better every time you saw him? Well, Jay does. I can see why Sky chose him. He's wearing blue jeans, a black button-down shirt, a fitted cap and a platinum chain. He also has a watch on with so many diamonds that its tough to look at. But what I really love is how he always smells like money. I'm pretty sure everything he has on is designer but I don't know much about labels - just the shit that Sky gives me.

"Why you got your clothes on?" he asks as he enters and slams the door. "I thought I told you I wanted that ass naked? You know I can't stay long."

He's pissed but I like it better when he takes my clothes off for me than for me to take them off myself. I have on my sexy black dress and, at $17 it deserves his full attention. As far as I'm concerned, to feel like a lady is worth hearing his fussing.

"Come on, Jay," I persist, locking the door then gently grabbing his hand. "I got my room all nice and pretty for you. I thought we could do it on the bed tonight."

"Listen, shawty," he snaps, snatching his hand from me, "I told you I'm not with all that romance shit. We straight fucking, that's it! When I come over here I want to see that ass naked and bent over on the sink. Fuck this dress and them rose petals and shit."

"I know it's just that..."

He cuts me off, grabs my face and says, "Don't fucking fall in love with me, Parade. You'll get your feelings hurt. Sky's the only woman for me."

I know I should be mad at how he grabs my face and yells hateful shit at me, but you know what I'm thinking? At least he's touching my face. With all my scars and all my bumps, he's still touching me. In a way, it makes me want to do something about my skin. Maybe next time he touches me, he'd see a clearer face and want me.

"I know, baby," I speak real softly. "I know it's not cool to fall in love with you, and I'll try my hardest not to. It's just that...I wanted to make things nice for you."

"Naw, later for that. Make shit nice for me by doing what the fuck I ask you."

"It wasn't any trouble. You can fuck me the same way you would over the sink, on my bed."

"Yeah, 'aight," he says as he follows me.

I have the candles lit, the room clean and the air fresh but he doesn't notice.

"Bend the fuck over and grab your ankles."

I bend over.

He unzips his pants, pulls up my dress and rips off my panties. Damn! There goes seven dollars down the drain. And for me that is a big deal, considering I ain't got no job.

The panty set I was wearing could be an electric fence, and he still wouldn't care. But with 10-inches of good hard dick with a nice mushroom shape head and thick vein running down the shaft, it is worth every minute. I do as he instructs and yell his name as if it matters. I feel his warm, hard rod inside me. Damn, fucking him always feels *sooo* good. As usual, I am imagining that I'm Sky, and that him and me live together and the sex feels even better.

"Take me, baby. It's all for you," I yell, backing up against his dick.

"I will, you black, ugly bitch. I'm gonna bang this black-ass ugly pussy out."

His comment brings me back to reality. I take a deep breath and a few harsh words then I'm black, ugly Parade again. Don't be alarmed. He always talks to me like that. Does it hurt? Yes, it does. But didn't I say this man is fine? And didn't I tell you I *am* ugly? I should be grateful he's even over here. I'll never get a man like this otherwise.

Honestly, I always wonder why he wastes his time on me and what he sees in me, besides the fact that I sex him the way he likes it. He can *fuck* anybody he wants. I know girls like me have to take what we can get. Daffany and Miss Wayne tell me I'm pretty all the time. They love my eyes and always compliment my smile. I don't believe them, though. Sky and my mother keep it real about how I look. They tell me the truth, so I won't go out here believing I'm anything but an ugly dark-skin girl. The only time I even consider believing Miss Wayne and Daffany is when Jay walks through my door. But, still, he eventually reminds me of who I am.

Anyway, this is how most men talk to me and, sometimes, it turns me on. Maybe, I feel like I am doing something for them their women won't. In my mind, they need to be with me. They need someone less attractive to make them feel appreciated and loved. To me, this is the caviar of sex and the Moet of life, and it can't get any better than this. And until my soul mate comes along, don't ask me to think otherwise.

"Get on your knees and open your mouth," he requests as he shakes his dick on the verge of busting a nut.

I get on my knees and open my mouth. I feel a big glob of his cum in the back of my throat.

"Ummmmm," I moan then swallow. "You taste so good."

He zips his pants, drops $50 on the counter and walks out. *I wonder how much Sky gets,* I think as I clean myself up.

CHAPTER 2

SKY TAYLOR

"Well, hurry the fuck up," I yell at my late ass boyfriend from my cell phone. "I've been waiting for over an hour on your bitch ass."

"Man, calm the fuck down," he screams. "I'm on my way."

I slam my pink RAZR cell phone shut and throw it in the passenger seat of my car. Here I am, sitting outside of Arundel Mills Mall in Maryland, waiting for my so-called man to meet me. We are supposed to be going to the movies and he's late. Although I want to stab his ass sometimes, he's everything to me. Well...he's everything to me *financially*. Lately, I have the strange feeling he's cheating on me. He comes late, talks to me how he wants to and doesn't want to fuck me that much. And trust me, I need dick like I need food and water. I can't tell you the number of times that I've gone to the store to replace my electronic butterfly vibrator just to bust a nut.

If I tell my friends I have to beg for sex from him they won't believe me. You don't understand. I'm Sky Taylor! The prettiest, sexiest and sassiest redbone known to man. When I walk in a room, everybody stops and looks, women included. If you see my best friends, especially Parade, you'll appreciate me walking into the room.

To say that girl is ugly is an understatement. They make pet asses that look better than her. I try to give her the clothes, I don't wear, but even top designers can't help that face of hers. And when we're out, I stand as close to her, as possible, so that my prettiness will rub off on her. I'm doing her a favor by being her friend. People ask me why all the time, too. I tell them straight up that we've lived together in ghetto-ass Quincy Manor apartments since we were kids. Outside of Miss Wayne and Daffany, I've known Parade all my life.

I'm like the diamond, and my friends are the rough. And it's easy to understand why, because my mother and father are both models. They're in their late thirties, and even now they stay out of town on assignments for Sean John, Roca wear and Baby Phat. We don't stay in the hood because we have to. We stay there because we can stash our money and buy the stuff we want and pay dirt cheap prices for rent. For now, I'm okay with where I live but, eventually, I do wanna leave — I just hope it's with Jay.

As I glance down at my Movado I realize 15 more minutes passed and he's still not here. I can only listen to so many CDs before I start getting irritated sitting in

Black and Ugly

this brand new red Honda Accord that he bought for me.

"Jay, you're late," I yell at him from my window as his white Yukon pulls up next to my car. "Where in the fuck have you been?"

"Look, I had business to take care of," he says as he gets out of his truck, slams the door and opens mine.

He has his own clothing store in DC, which is a front for the drug operation he runs. Money is not a problem. One thing I can say about him is this, if he thinks he's hurt me then he'll drop money on me in a heartbeat. Watch this.

"Did it really take you all night?" I ask, getting out of my car and turning on the alarm.

"Yes, it did."

He reaches in and kisses me. *Mmmmm.* His lips are always so sweet.

"If I don't run my shit," he continues, "how you gonna get all that loot I give you?"

"What kind of business you got tonight that's so important it couldn't wait? You know I hate to be late, and the movie's about to start. I was sitting in my car by myself, Jay. What if somebody tried to hurt me? You had me looking stupid for over an hour."

"You survived, Sky."

"Yeah, but you know these dudes out here were trying to holla at me, right?" I'm lying, but I know it will piss him off.

"Come on, Sky. Why you always gotta give me shit? I'm here now, 'aight? And if you wanted them weak ass niggas — 'cuz I'm sure they were some bitches trying to holla at a girl in a car — then you shoulda went with 'em."

He's mad, but I knew he would be. He looks sexy when he's mad too. Just looking at this black-and-Latin mixed mothafucka makes anybody wanna say, Neva mind. I ain't even mad no more.

"Well it's obvious you don't give a fuck about my feelings," I whine. "I might as well go home," I continue like I am getting ready to cry and walk back to my car.

"Aight, ma, you got it," he says as he grabs me. "Hold out your hand." He's reaching in his pocket for the roll.

I love the roll. When he comes to my house and puts it on my dresser next to the bed where we make love, I admire it when he goes to sleep. I pick it up, feel it, smell it and pretend it is all mine.

Black and Ugly

"Okay," I say with my arms folded, pretending I ain't wanna hear nothing he is trying to say. But when he peels off $500, I can't help but smile.

"Thanks, daddy," I chime as he bends down, kisses me, and I gently grab his dick. "You know I'm hitting that in the theater, right?"

"Hell yeah, girl." He touches my face gently with his hand. I take one of his fingers and place it in my mouth rotating my tongue around it. It drives him crazy. I smell a faint odor and figure he didn't wash his hands.

"Damn, Sky," he says looking into my eyes. "I broke my neck to get over here to you. That's the only reason I stay coming with you to the movies. I don't give a fuck what be playing. You trying to get a nigga sprung," he continues as he grabs my ass. "I'm feeling that outfit, too, ma. That shits hot. Don't have me break a nigga's jaw out here for staring at yo ass."

"Boy, stop playing." I blush.

I am giving it up too. He ain't lying and I love when he gets a little violent by threatening to beat my ass and shit. It only means he cares. Men don't trip unless they feel threatened or are afraid they may lose you. That's right, baby. Get a good look at this ass so you can see what you'll miss if you fuck up.

We walk through Arundel Mills Mall toward the theater and all eyes are on us. The atmosphere at night is more like a club than anything, partially because Dave and Buster's is inside the mall too. We really do look like a fly ass couple. I have on my three-quarter-inch boots and my one-piece sleeveless black jumper, which complements my calves, cleavage and ass. I completed my look with the Tiffany diamond collection set Jay bought me, which included the earrings, necklace, bracelet and ring. The niggas is on me and the bitches is on him. The haters are on the sidelines hating as usual. I kinda like the haters, though. They let you know you're really doing the damn thing.

"You get the tickets, ma?"

"Yeah, papi. I know you hate standing in line," I tell him as I grab his hand to let the redbone in the corner staring know that this one belongs to me. See, I ain't worried about the darkies 'cuz Jay hates chocolate. He once told me a dark-skin girl can't even get his dick hard. But them redbones, he loves with a passion.

Black and Ugly

We move through the theater, it's packed, and people are everywhere. I hate going to see a movie on opening night, but I love the attention. We are elbow to elbow with people we don't know. And now, they are so close that nobody can really see my outfit.

We are waiting in the line to get some snacks, this one dude behind me is staring me down like I am the last chicken wing on the plate. He has his girl with him and everything or maybe it's his wife, who knows? He ain't even looking at my face, just focusing on my body and my ass. I turn around slightly, pretending to give a fuck about how crowded the line is behind me, so he can get a good look at me. I want him to see I'm a total package.

I recognize him from around the way. He smiles, suggesting he recognizes me too. I'm sure he knows who I am because I'm definitely popular, but for some reason, I can't remember his name. If my memory serves me correctly, he is the owner of a 2006 silver Mercedes Benz CLS55 with charcoal interior.

He doesn't live in the Manor, but I see him coming through from time to time. He probably has business with the dealers, I'm sure. Outside of his car, I can tell he is caked up by the looks of his chick. She has diamonds so big that they put my Tiffany set to shame, and trust me; it is hard to put my set to shame. The thing that really cracks my neck is the canary yellow, diamond pendant necklace she's flossing. I can also tell her tracks are laid professionally because they move every time she does. Bitch! You can always tell how good a nigga's eating by the bitch he puts on his arm.

Maybe, I'm mad or, maybe, I just want to start shit but I'm about to fuck with him a little. Plus, if he sees me again, I want him to know that he has an open invitation to approach me. With Jay acting up lately, I can never tell how long he'll be around. Who knows, maybe this dude can be my other option? I mean, Jay takes care of me because I damn sure ain't got no job but lately, he's been slacking in the attention department.

"What you doing, girl?" Jay says, sensing I am up to something.

"Nothing, baby," I lie as I reach for a kiss and put one finger through the belt loop on his jeans.

I look at the line ahead of me and see there are three people in front of us. Our server is extremely slow, and this is the only time I am happy with poor service. It gives me time to play out my game a little.

I should feel bad because Jay stay putting niggas in their place when we go out. One time I cut up and he

30   *Black and Ugly*

had to pull his heat out on this dude. But for some reason, I don't care about starting shit tonight. As far as I'm concerned, I'm keeping him on his toes. He needs to be reminded that he is lucky to be with me. I'm a bad bitch, and he knows it.

I'm seductively swaying my hips to get the other man's attention, as if that's hard to do. You know, like I'm so tired of standing in the line that I gotta move otherwise I'll drive myself crazy. It's working, too, because I turn around to say, "This place is getting more and more packed, Jay," just to prevent him from suspecting something else," and dude is still looking at me.

"Let's go to the line over there. It's shorter," his girl says. I guess she can't take it no more. But he can, because he says, "Naw, we good right here."

Just for that bitch, I'ma do extra. I drop the ticket stub on the floor and bend down real slowly to pick it up. My ass is inches away from her man's dick. Even though it's packed, I can tell he *wants* to be really close to me because he doesn't move.

"Damn," he says real low, but loud enough for me to hear him.

I didn't expect him to say that. I would knock Jay out for that shit.

"I'ma smack one of these freak bitches in here," she mumbles as she walks away.

He follows her, asking her what's wrong. Poor thing. She don't even know how to keep her man in check. And smacking me? I wish she would. I'd beat her ass.

"What you want, ma?" Jay asks as he wraps his arm around my waist and pulls me closer to him at the concession stand.

He must know I'm up to something. He tells me all the time I need to get along with women, more, and stop being so catty.

"Somebody gonna fuck you up one day," he use to tell me. "Mark my words."

I thought that was funny because Parade would stomp somebody out for fucking with me. All I have to do is give the word, and it's on. Besides, I told him I got along with women just fine. But, I was talking about Miss Wayne, Daffany and Parade. He said they didn't count because they look up to me. But what was wrong with that?

Anyway, I love when he grabs me instead of me grabbing him all the time when we're out in public. This way I don't look all insecure and pressed.

"Umm…I just want a soda."

"You don't want no popcorn? You must be bugging."

"No, boy. I ate at home. Mommy made a big ass meal, fried chicken and everything."

32　　　　　*Black and Ugly*

I'm lying, again. She did cook but I didn't eat because there was no way I was squeezing my ass into this outfit with a potbelly. He reaches down kisses me again and fucked up feeling comes over me. I smell him. What is that scent?

"Jay, what you wearing?"

He acts like he doesn't hear me, but I know he do. People are not talking so loud that he can't hear me. This only makes me more suspicious.

"Jay! What are you wearing?" I yell, reminding him that I'm the same ghetto bitch he met in the mall parking lot two years ago, who don't mind acting real stupid if provoked.

"Girl, I don't know. Deodorant. Why?" he snaps, all pissed off and shit.

He grabs his popcorn and hands me my soda. We are in the movie theater and I remember exactly where I know the smell. It's the BeBe perfume I gave Parade on account of her asking me for it over and over. She wears it everyday. I use to love that perfume, too but she wore it so much, that it started to remind me of her. Cheap. It was a catalog purchase, so ain't a lot of girls got it.

I grab his shirt and sniff it again.

"What you doing, girl?" He yells, like I give a fuck. "Stop acting dumb and watch the movie."

"Whatever, you sneaky mothafucka," I yell back.

The smell on his clothes almost makes me queasy. I'm happy the theater is dark, because it helps me to play shit out in my head. I mean, why would he be with Parade? He hates black bitches. *But,* why is the smell so strong on his shirt? Maybe it's another girl. Yeah, it has to be another girl. *I should slap the fuck out of him right now.* I cut my eyes at him.

"What, girl?" he says as he gives me the look that usually means he's getting ready to fuck me up. "Stop tripping and watch the movie."

"Fuck that movie," I shout back.

I don't think he'd fuck with Parade. Her body is nice, but her skin is fucked up because she doesn't take care of her shit. Miss Wayne gave her some of that Proactiv stuff a while back to clear up her face. I told her I knew somebody who used it and it didn't work so she never tried. It's probably still in the box right now.

I thought Miss Wayne was wrong for that shit because Parade will always be black, and she will always be ugly. And that makes me feel better, 'cuz I can't imagine Jay fucking with her. But just to be sure, I'm gonna ask Parade what she did tonight. Don't get me wrong. She ain't no competition, but I'm thinking about what they say, pussy ain't got no face. I sure hope that ain't true.

CHAPTER 3

MISS WAYNE

Okay something's real conspicuous about these bitches. What the fuck is going on in here? We all riding *together* in the same car, but for real...you'd never know.

I can tell something is on Parade's mind because she's picking a scab on her face and, now, the pink shows under her skin. I tap her on the shoulder to get her to stop and, on queue she drops her hands in her lap. She only picks at her face when she's nervous and something is on her mind.

"Parade...maybe you shouldn't have worn those tennis with that outfit," Miss Sky says, waking her out of her trance. "You ain't have nothing else to put on?"

Now Miss Sky is acting like a bitch, 'cuz she knows that chile ain't got shit in her closet to wear besides the stuff she already gave her. That don't make no damn sense. She's been ragging on that girl ever since we were in elementary school. It's a sight to see. Just plain old pitiful. I wish Miss Parade would stand up for herself and cuss Miss Sky out. I'll pay money to see that shit, chile. I've seen this girl stomp out three and four bitches at a time. But, whenever Miss Sky confronts her, she becomes defenseless.

"No," Miss Parade responds, staring at the road. "These the only ones that fit. I got some money on me, though," she continues, glancing at Sky briefly then looking at the road again. "Maybe I'll buy a new pair instead of buying an outfit for the party tomorrow night."

"Miss Parade, if you short, baby, I'll front you," I tell her.

"Thanks, Miss Wayne, but you gave me some money already."

"Well, you need to let somebody do something, 'cuz I ain't walking into that party with your hair looking like shit. You look like you fucking homeless or something. And don't ask me for no money, either, because I'm tired of giving it to you," Miss Sky continues as she combs through her own curly hair with her fingers, making sure each strand is perfect.

"Ooooo, bitch, what has gotten into you? How dare you make Miss Parade feel that way when you know the situation," I yell.

See, I don't give a fuck if it's her car or not. I'll turn this mothafucka out.

"Yeah, Sky, you acting a little funky today. We all going to the mall and if we have to, we'll put in money to make sure Parade got something tight to throw on

Black and Ugly

tomorrow. What she got on her feet right now ain't bothering nobody. Now it's a nice day, let's not ruin it," Miss Daffany says from the backseat with me.

Miss Parade is silent as usual but stops picking her face. Miss Sky, although mad as hell, doesn't say shit else to none of us. We get to the mall; she parks the car, gets out and walks into Arundel Mills like we ain't even with her. But, I want her to walk ahead so I can get the "T" or 411 from Miss Parade.

"Miss Daffany, go with her, chile. I wanna talk to Miss Parade alone."

"Okay," she says as she looks up at Miss Sky, "but you know I hate having Sky duty."

"For me, precious," I say, flashing a smile.

"For both of ya'll," she responds, referring to Miss Parade and me.

"What's going on, baby? Why that bitch throwing you shade?" I ask as we sit down in the food court area while Miss Sky and Miss Daffany walk into The Gap.

"She always do that. You know how she is," Miss Parade responds.

"And that makes it right?"

"No...but I don't like to get her upset with me. Plus, you know what I'm doing is wrong," she says as she looks down on the ground. "With Jay and all."

"That's true, baby, but Miss Thang is extra today. I am but five seconds from slapping the sound out of her right ear."

She laughs, and I'm happy I can make her smile. Miss Parade has a beautiful smile, but shies away from compliments, so I avoid telling her as much as I like to.

"I'm serious, honey. I was gonna slap some sense into her ass," I continue.

"Don't do that. She does so much for me. I just wish she'd stop treating me all fucked up and shit, especially around ya'll."

"Well, we family, baby. Like you said, we already know how the bitch is."

"But it's still embarrassing," she continues. "Whenever she mad at something or someone, she takes it out on me."

"Well, say something then, Miss Parade. She ain't gonna stop unless you say something to her. She ain't nothing but a bully. A big ole meany with horns," I say as I hit the table. "We in our twenties, and she still doing the same shit she did to you in elementary. I don't even see how ya'll stayed friends so long. Hell, I don't see how I stayed friends with the bitch so long." I laugh.

"Eventually I'll say something to her," she whispers.

"You want me to?"

Black and Ugly

"No...then she'll really fuck with me 'cuz she'll know she's getting to me."

"Okay," I say, mad at the missed opportunity to put Miss Sky in her place, "but you don't have a clue what's wrong this time? Because by the way she acting, I'd think something else was up."

"I don't know, Miss Wayne. She called me today and asked me what I do last night. I told her I saw Melvin and she picked me up and been acting funny ever since."

"Well, did you see Melvin last night?"

"No," she says and pauses. "I can't stand his ass no more. I was with Jay for a minute. It was right before they went to the movies too. But I don't know how she could know that."

"Oooooh. That's what it is, girl. Maybe she found out."

"Doubt it."

"Can you really be sure?" I ask, understanding why Miss Sky is so mad.

"I didn't tell her anything. I don't even want him seeing me right before he sees her. And I know Jay ain't saying shit. He don't even like admitting he likes dark-skin girls."

"You right 'bout that. Like something's wrong with a piece of chocolate. Hell, I'm a red man, and I loves me the chocolate boys, girl." I laugh.

"But, he says he isn't attracted to dark-skin women," she responds, unmoved by my comment.

I know it bothers her that she is dark skin but, really, she is gorgeous. It seems like as the years went by, her cheekbones became more defined while her eyes widened and the scars, from the fights she'd been in all her life, started to slowly fade. If she stop picking the bumps from the slight acne problem she has, she'll feel better about herself. But no matter how beautiful her eyes are and how gorgeous her smile appears, she is always sad. Miss Daffany and me believe that if she get her skin together, she can even be a model, but she doesn't listen to us. She thinks we feel sorry for her and is unwilling to tell the truth, like her stupid ass mother and Miss Sky. But that is hardly the case.

Her wretched ass, jealous mother does a world of damage by telling her how unattractive she is everyday she wakes up. When we were in elementary school, she came in our class and took a hat off Miss Parade's head, revealing the choppy hairstyle she gave her the night before. She claimed she was looking for the hat and didn't know Parade had it on, but all she did was torture the girl.

"I hear what you saying, baby, but Miss Sky is wrong—just plain old wrong—chile. And that's why I'm glad you fucking her man. Miss Sky went overboard today, and that chile has smelled her own ass for far too long and she still don't think it stinks. So you do you, and don't worry with nothing else."

"Thanks, Miss Wayne," she says with a slight smile but I can tell she still feels guilty for sleeping with Jay.

"But, may I make a suggestion honey?"

"Sure," she says.

"It don't make no sense you fucking that rich ass nigga and you ain't got enough money to buy a decent pair of shoes. Jay should be paying you at least half of what Miss Sky is getting, chile, if not more."

"I know," she responds, feeling embarrassed, "but I'm not his girl."

"But here's the thing. A man won't give you shit unless you ask him for it. You gotta make him feel like you deserve it, because you do. And then the money will come from everywhere, honey. Oooooh, girl, you'd have so many coins, you could buy your own fly shit, and stop taking what Miss Sky gives you." I laugh. "You think Miss Sky gotta ask Jay ass for shit, now?" I pause. "Hell no."

She looks down toward the ground again, and this time I can tell she is on the verge of crying. "He ain't spending no real money on me. What we have is just sexual."

"Why should he spend anything on you? You act like you don't deserve nothing but you do, baby. You do deserve it," I say as I lift her head up. "Make his ass pay. Don't no pussy grow on trees, including yours."

She looks sad, but I need to tell her the truth. Miss Parade has been passing out free pussy for far too long. I have to put an end to that shit.

"I'm not good with asking men for money. I don't even see how she does it."

"Honey, I *dooos* it too. You do it just like this: You looks 'em up and down while they dicks in they hands and say, 'Ain't shit in life free so leave $200 on the table, please.'"

"I'm serious," she grins.

"And so am I! You gotta pay the waiter after dinner is served, don't you?"

She nods.

"Well, there you go."

She's laughing, and I am happy because Miss Sky broke her down lower than a hoe with no legs earlier in the car today.

"I'll try."

"Yeah, you better, gurl."

As we finish talking, Miss Sky and Miss Daffany rejoin us. Apparently Miss Sky isn't mad no more because she is finally talking to Miss Parade. I guess Miss Daffany told her about herself and this is her way of apologizing.

"So we can go to LVLX to get you something to put on, and you can grab some shoes in Off Broadway shoe store," Miss Sky commands.

"Thanks, Sky. I have $50 to put to everything too," Miss Parade obliges.

"Keep that for your hair. I made appointments for us, with Carol, when I was in the store."

"Well what about me?" I ask. "I needs to find me something to wear, too, now. Y'all ain't gonna be the only bitches flossing tomorrow night."

"Bitch, you betta spend your own money." Miss Sky laughs.

"Why spend mine when I can spend yours?" I sass her.

"And what are you wearing anyway?" Miss Daffany asks.

"I don't know yet. The possibilities are endless, chile. Look at me. Could I look bad in anything?" We all start laughing in the middle of the mall.

See let me tell you something 'bout me. I'm gorgeous, baby. Like right now, I'm wearing my silk pants, cowboy boots, red silk shirt and a touch of clear lip-gloss. My hair is smoothed back with a lil' bit of gel and, trust me darlings, I look fierce.

I like hanging out with my girls because they draw attention. See, faggies are jealous and sneaky and I don't need all that shit around me. Especially when I know, I'm sneaky too. I got one faggy friend I deal with for business purposes only and that's Miss Rick. My other friend is Taylor and although he's in the life, meaning he likes men, he doesn't act all wild and crazy like some gays. But, most of the time, it's only business related. Now if I hung out with every faggy on the street, I'd get into too much trouble. But my girls, I've known them all my life. I trust them with my men and they trust me with theirs. I fuck the ones they don't want and warn them about the ones I want. It works out perfectly because I only inform them about the ones I knew were gay anyway.

We finish shopping and Miss Parade has two outfits and two pairs of shoes while everybody else is loaded up and ready to go. I'm happy that Miss Sky dropped the money she did on Miss Parade. After all, the money is rightfully Miss Parade's, too, considering they're sleeping with the same man.

Now, Miss Parade fucking Jay may be wrong but if it wasn't her, it would be somebody else. Jay ain't no good, grant it but Miss Parade snagging him proves my point that she can have any man she wants. Miss Sky being light skin ain't got nothing to do with it. It's all about personality. She doesn't have to stick with the short and stubby Melvin look alikes just because she hasn't learned to appreciate her complexion.

If you ask me, I think Jay's fucked Miss Daffany, too, but she'd never admit it. She don't give no names, of the men she fucks in the Manor, even when we beg her. She says, "I don't give out the names of my clients." So we stop asking. Probably because they'd fuck her up if they find out. Most of them are married so they're sleeping with her right under their wives' noses. I know I saw Jay crawling out of the same hole she did one day but I could be wrong.

"Did you see that bitch's hair? It was a mess." Miss Sky laughs on the way out the mall's door.

We turn around, but must've missed the girl she's talking about because the one I see is attractive. Miss Sky's a troublemaker, always keeping up shit. Since I've been knowing her, she's started at least 50 fights and got all of our asses locked up one night.

"What you say, bitch?" the attractive girl says. I'm not surprised. "I know you ain't talking about nobody's hair," she continues as she and her friend approach us.

Despite the evil look on her face, she is a pretty little thing. Looks like somebody's trophy for real. She has the Chinese cut with the spiky bangs and it's her natural hair, falling all the way down her back. She's killing that cut. So truthfully, I don't think Miss Sky was talking 'bout her, but at this point, it doesn't even matter.

"Get out my face, bitch," Miss Sky says as she moves toward the door. Of course, Miss Parade appears to give her cover.

Miss Parade was on it. She dropped her bags and was ready to handle shit the moment the girl opened her mouth. She assumed her position like she always did, in front of Sky. It's almost as if she's her personal bodyguard or something.

"And what the fuck you wanna do?" the attractive woman asks Miss Parade. "Your friend real comical, talking about somebody's hair when yours look like some shit. Did you comb that shit or just gel it?"

She has some girls with her and all are pointing and laughing at Miss Parade's hair. But, Miss Parade ain't say nothing. She use to tell us, all the time, that she can tell who's scared by how much shit they talk when it's time to fight. She believes if they are really 'bout it, they won't be running their mouth.

She is always ready to fight, and for real, I think she loves it. She told me that the reason she's won every battle is because she goes to a different place mentally. She thinks about every person who has ever done her wrong and takes it all out on her victim. All I know is whatever she does it works. "Listen, sweetie, why don't you wiggle your little ass on down the mall 'cuz it is not that serious," I tell the bitch, honestly, trying to prevent Miss Parade from getting out on her.

"Are you serious? Aren't you a little too big for those pants? What are you extra large and they're an extra small? What possessed you to think…" the bitch utters.

"Bitch, shut the fuck up. I wasn't even talking to your simple ass anyway," Miss Sky retorts, "but just for stepping over here, you getting ready to get fucked up."

"You wish, bitch," she argues as she moves closer to us with Miss Parade silent and in Miss Sky's way.

By T. Styles   47

Miss Daffany grabs everybody's bags and tucks them behind this trashcan in the corner. Although we are getting ready to get down, we all have our peripheral vision glued to our gear in case somebody tried to take it. I know if that blueberry-colored top, I just bought, was stolen, there'd be a series of ass whippings in this mothafucka today.

"Look…I'ma tell you one more time to get the fuck down the mall. You don't want none of this for real," Miss Daffany yells.

By now, it's five girls with them and five girls with us because, when Miss Parade goes off, chile, she makes two.

"Fuck you, bitch," the girl says.

Miss Parade steals the fuck out of her. She fights like a man and her punches are powerful. The girl tries to get up and starts swinging her arms wildly, but Miss Parade steals her ass again since her face is wide open.

"That's how you fight, bitch?" Miss Parade asks as she hit her again, this time with a two-piece, extra crispy. "You ain't nothing but a joke."

The funny part about it is that her friends don't help. Blood from her mouth is dripping all over her clothes and on the floor. She's trying to get a lick in, but she ain't no match for Miss Parade. One of her wild-arm throws comes across Miss Parade's face and she is pissed. Miss Daffany steps up to help, and the girl's friends are already running toward the door. We ain't have shit to do but watch.

"Don't jump in, Daf. I got this bitch," Miss Parade tells her.

We fall back and watch her as she damn near Laila Ali's the girl. It's almost scary to watch—*almost*. None of us feel bad for not jumping in. Sky should but doesn't. But, Miss Parade needs no help. Hell, she once beat two girls back to back in school.

That day, she started out fighting one person when another girl decided she would stop it by holding Miss Parade. When she did that, it gave the first girl a chance to hit Miss Parade in her face.

Miss Parade waited until after school for the girl who stole her. She whipped that girl's ass like she stole her man. And then knocked on the other girl's door to beat her unmercifully. When I asked her why the girl, who held her back, got beat worse, she said she hates when somebody holds her back and loves a good fight.

People are crowding around now and we see the mall cops coming, so we snatch Miss Parade's black ass up off the girl who is now on the ground and get the fuck out of dodge. It really is pitiful to see somebody getting stomped out like that but we warned her. Me, Miss Sky and Miss Daffany are laughing and talking about the fight all the way home.

I look at Miss Parade in the passenger seat and she ain't laughing at all. She has her hands on her face in preparation to pick her skin again. I think, in her mind, there is nothing funny about having another scar on her face. Poor thang.

CHAPTER 4

DAFFANY STANS

My life is different than it was five months ago. I laughed at all the money I was getting from these dudes back then. Although I turned tricks, I believed they were dumb for paying for sex, but I wasn't dumb for supplying their needs. I was simply making cash off their weaknesses. The thing is, most of them didn't even have to pay for sex but they did anyway. They had wives and girlfriends, who were more than willing to do everything I do if they just asked. Hell, most of their women are bigger freaks than me.

But they didn't want them to fulfill their sexual fantasies; they wanted me to. My price was high. And now, I realize that they don't pay for the sex as much as they pay for the ability to leave without emotion, without feelings attached. I stacked their cash and laughed with my friends about the things they wanted me to do, while never naming names.

Yeah, five months ago was definitely different. I looked forward to days and spending time with my friends, the only real family I have. But, I don't care what I do anymore and, now, I have no real purpose. All I ever succeeded at doing was making a real fuck up of my life and even if I wanted to get out, now I can't.

I moved out of the apartment I shared with my moms and got my own in the same development, but she stays over my place more than she does hers. Bumming all the time and borrowing shit that she never gives back. She pawned five of my vacuum cleaners I continued to let her borrow and that was one of the main reasons I moved. My mother smokes so much crack that I don't know how she even pays her bills but, then, I remember we're in the same line of work. As a matter of fact, we have some of the same customers. In the back of my mind, I wonder if it was her that gave it to me. Hell, she gave me the game by always telling me that if I wanted or needed anything there's some sucka out here who would give it to me, that I better get mine like she gets hers. She lived by the rule - fuck you...pay me - which she'll tell a nigga in a heartbeat. I didn't know any other way of getting money. Besides, I wasn't tied to these no good ass niggas, so I had the best of both worlds – money and dick with no one to report to. But, my world has shattered and I'm curious if the doctor told her the same thing that he told me.

What am I talking about?

Black and Ugly

"Daffany Stans, you're HIV positive," Doctor Scott told me. I screamed and cried for 15 minutes in his office, trying to convince him to change the results. "Take it back! Take it back," I pleaded with him. I was so delusional that I thought he could change my life by, simply saying it wasn't true or that he made a mistake as oppose to thinking about all the men I slept with without a condom 'cuz they was willing to pay a few more dollars.

I told him there was no way I was positive. I wasn't even sick. After he told me over and over that he couldn't lie to me and threatened to call security, I decided he must've gotten my results mixed up with someone else's. "Look at the name over again," I demand. But then, he handed me the paper with the name I've known all my life on it. Damn! It was definitely Daffany Stans.

I've always been quiet, but more so over the last few months. Sky says when you're quiet people think you're sneaky. Maybe, it's true. But lately, I feel like there's even less shit to talk about. I can't laugh knowing that, in the end, nothing is funny. I will always have fucking HIV. The little things that are important to everybody else are not important to me anymore. I'm a walking zombie just waiting for my number to be up. And if it wasn't for my friends, I'd be gone already.

By T. Styles   53

Parade thinks she has troubles because she isn't the most attractive person in the world. I would trade shoes with her in a heartbeat. She's not even unattractive. She makes herself ugly because she don't take care of her skin and or have the slightest idea of what to do with her hair. She has pretty eyes, a pretty smile and a beautiful complexion but every time me, and Miss Wayne, tell her, she just rolls her eyes at us. So, I don't tell her anymore. I got problems of my fucking own now and, that's all I can think about.

"Oooooh, Miss Daffany. Girl, that outfit is looking fierce. I don't know if I can let you get in here with us wearing that. Miss Sky, pull off, girl." Miss Wayne laughs from the inside of the car.

When I get in, everybody's smelling and looking good. Sky had taken Parade to the salon she went to in DC and even she looks nice. The short curls, in her hair, soften her features and bring out her beauty. She has makeup on and everything.

"Don't hold back, bitches," I say as I get in the car and smell the weed. "Pass that shit around."

Black and Ugly

Weed and E-pills are the only things that make me feel normal. On E, I don't have a care in the world. I popped before I left the house and I'm starting to feel a little better. I didn't tell them that I fucked with the E because, sometimes, they act all bourgeois and shit when it comes to Ecstasy, talking about people be lunching out on that shit. What Sky doesn't know is that I buy all my pills from Jay, and depending on how much money I have and what he wants, I don't have to pay. Every now and again, he'll pop one with me.

"Here you go, girl," Miss Wayne says as he passes the bob. "So what time does it start, Miss Sky? I can't be cooped up, too long, with this outfit on. This thing's made for watching."

"It started at 10:30, so we're about an hour late. But we don't wanna be the first ones there anyway. We gotta make an entrance," Sky adds.

"Who giving it?" Parade questions.

"Donna. She throwing it at her mom's house in DC," Sky answers.

"Uuuggh. You know she fucks with Silver's cousin, right?" I ask Sky. "I can't stand them crooks."

"I was thinking the same thing, girl," Parade says to Miss Wayne. "I hope Silver and them ain't coming either. They start too much shit."

"Girl, who gives a fuck if Silver and them coming or not?" Sky says. "Silver and them are caked up. And

By T. Styles   55

somebody in your position shouldn't be choosy anyway, Parade. If you were smart you'd be trying to fuck with one of them. You always hating, throwing monkey wrenches in shit," Sky continues.

She comes down on Parade hard as cold dog shit, all the time. If me, or Miss Wayne, said something about it every time she did it, we'd never get along. Plus, Sky doesn't have to hang with any of us, but she does. Besides, she's the only one in the group with a car. I mean, everybody know that I fuck for money, Miss Wayne is a faggy and Parade ain't the cutest thing but she never cuts us off.

"Well, I hope they don't come in and fuck shit up either," Miss Wayne interjects. "At least not before I meets my new baby daddy. Plus, I'm still mad at them for robbing me."

"You ain't got no proof they did it," Sky says.

"No proof?" Miss Wayne repeats as he moves his hands back and forth in disbelief. He is so extra, but it's always funny to see. "No proof? Bitch, Markee's young ass dropped his school ID on my living room floor. What more proof I need, chile? I woulda called the cops, if all that shit wasn't stolen anyway."

Girlfriend is so funny. That is his way of taking some of the heat off Parade and putting it on himself. He's always there for her. Car or not, Sky don't give us half of the shit she gives Parade. And you can get Miss

Wayne wrong if you want to but he's liable to stab you. He's the only faggy in the neighborhood the niggas tolerated.

See, Miss Wayne once slashed a nigga's face for calling him a faggy in front of his mamma, after he sucked his dick the day before. Once he did that shit, he gained respect from the dudes around the way. He did it because he thinks faggy's are stupid and he'll tell you, quick, "I'm far from stupid, darling."

But try asking him what's the difference between being gay and being a faggy, you'll be even more confused. Although he hates outsiders to call him a faggy, I've heard him use it with the few gay guys he hangs around. I guess it's like the word *nigga* among blacks. Some people simply can't use it. Miss Wayne ain't no small dude either. He's real light skin and looks more like a body builder than anything else. Sound okay? Well, imagine a body builder in pumps and spandex dresses with a purse. Exactly! But, I fucks with him 'cuz he keeps it real.

The party is crowded and you can barely move, and the stereo rattles the windows throughout the house. People were popping and I am trying to scope the room to see who I can get mine from.

"Girl, this shit is terrible. We shoulda went to club Love," Parade says.

"I hate Love. This alright, girl. You gotta get some liquor up in you, that's all."

I'm kicking it with Parade when just as I suspected, Silver and his friends walk in, and they are already starting shit.

"You see 'em, right?" Parade asks.

"Yeah, girl. Damn we can't neva go nowhere without them being around," I co-sign.

"It's these neighborhood shindigs. We gotta branch out and stop hanging with people 'round our way."

Parade is talking but I am not listening because I'm trying to see who came in with Silver and them. They are already spread out and looking for shit to get into. I hate them stupid ass niggas with a passion. They do everything from sticking people up to raping girls. The only reason people deal with them is so they'd leave them alone.

They haven't been at the party five minutes and already Markee, the youngest, smacks a girl because she doesn't wanna give him her number. That's how they are, and that's how they act all the time. Jackie, one of the brothers, came to me a month ago and wanted a blowjob. After I spent 30 minutes on this mothafucka, he jetted out without paying me my money. And then he had the nerve to speak to me the next day. But you can't do nothing about it because when you fuck with one, you fuck with all of 'em. So, instead of pressing him about my money, I took it as an L.

"Girl, that dude over there wanna holla at you," Sky says as she walks over to me.

It's the first time she came back since we got here an hour ago. She has two sets of friends and although we've known her the longest, she sometimes treats us like we are charity cases. If Jewel, her other friend who owns a beauty salon, is anywhere we are together, she'll leave us until it's time to go home.

Sky can be real shady when she wants to. So, as usual, I'm with Parade holding up the food table, and Miss Wayne is somewhere probably blowing some trade off. Now that Sky wants something, she's coming back.

See Sky tried to trick me off to dudes before, and at first I ain't mind. But then, she started doing it like I worked for her or something, saying shit like, "I got a job for you tomorrow, be ready." She had a lot of fucking nerve. So, I put an end to that shit quick. If we as tight as she say we are, she shouldn't be doing that shit. I learned from it quick, not to mix business with friendship. So, I told her the last time that I wasn't with that shit and she ain't talk to me for a month. Now, I know she knows better than to run game on me tonight.

"Naw. I think he with Silver, and you know I ain't fucking with them stupid ass niggas," I respond.

"No, he ain't, Daffany. You think everybody in here with them. I told him I know you, and he wants to holla. Now you gonna make me look like I don't know what I'm talking about," Sky says. "He seems real nice."

"Nice, huh?" I ask, looking her over.

"Yeah."

"Well I don't want to be bothered, Sky." I ain't sure but I can tell her sneaky ass is up to something. "Tell him I got a boyfriend or something."

"I already told him you didn't. And just 'cuz he talk to Silver don't mean he hang with him. Why don't you like them anyway?"

"Does it really matter? Silver and them is not as cool with everybody like they are with you. I don't got no boyfriend they're scared of."

"Just like I thought, you ain't got no reason," Sky says.

"I have my reasons but mainly 'cuz they act stupid."

I didn't tell her that one of them stiffed me for my dough after I sucked his dick. My friends know what I do, but don't know who I do it with. With me finding out I got HIV, I'm glad I never opened my mouth to anybody, including my friends. All I need is one of these niggas looking for me every time they get a cough and shit.

"Yeah...she's right, Sky. Silver's boys act too stupid. Markee just hit that girl over there 'cuz she ain't wanna give him her number. What is he even doing here? He's like a kid," Parade says as she sipped on her drink.

"First off, Parade, I'm not talking to you," Sky snaps, pointing her finger in her face. "You wouldn't be saying shit if somebody was trying to holla at your tired black ass," Sky continues.

Parade is taking deep breaths. See, I've seen her stomp bitches out for pointing their finger in her face. So letting Sky slide proves she takes a lot from her.

"Sky...get your fucking finger out my face."

Sky must know Parade ain't playing because she quickly withdraws her finger.

"You just jealous, Parade," she responds in a lower tone. "And that don't make no damn sense."

"Whatever. Just because I don't look a certain way don't mean I'm jealous of you. And there are plenty of dudes who still want me, no matter how you think I look. Trust me," Parade says. "You don't even know the half."

"And what the fuck is that supposed to mean?"

"It's supposed to mean exactly what I said," Parade yells.

Aw shit. Parade is finally getting buck with Sky. She never, ever talked back to her that way. For one, Sky would threaten not to do stuff for her anymore and, for two, Sky is the flyest friend Parade has.

I'm ordinary and I'm cool with it. I know about the labels, but I prefer to wear Express and spend more money on my shoes and purses than anything else. I'm brown skin, and I wear my hair in ponytails most of the time. I got really big breast and a flat ass. I think there's Chinese somewhere in my family 'cuz I have chinky eyes; although, my moms keep saying it ain't true. She's slept with too many men to count and probably don't know who my father is anyway.

"You know what, you little bitch, see the next time I do anything for you," Sky yells to Parade over the music.

To say Parade looks up to Sky is an understatement but, eventually, everybody gets tired being shitted on. All she's gonna do now is carry Parade and not answer the phone when she calls. Parade can't handle the heat from Sky when she throws her shade. She'd call me, or Miss Wayne, and beg us to talk to Sky for her. But Sky won't come around until she gets ready.

"Look...it's not that serious," I say as I grab Sky's hand. "She was taking up for me, that's all. I'll talk to him real quick, Sky. It's not a problem."

"First off...you don't need nobody taking up for you. We ain't kids. We grown-ass women," Sky says as she looks at Parade.

"Well maybe you should act like it," Parade responds with most of her mouth in her drink.

"I'm coming, Sky, dang. Just leave it alone."

"Okay," she says with an attitude. "*Anyway*...he's been asking about you all night, and I think you'll like him," she adds as she *play* hit me on my arm. "I'm trynna find you a man so you don't have to trick no more."

"Why you gotta say dumb shit, Sky? I don't need no man, and I'm not gonna stop tricking till the fuck I get ready to."

"Unless you a dyke, we all need a man." Sky laughs. "Well, he's feeling you. He's asked me about you all night," she resumes as we approach him while he's kicking it with one of his boys.

"Excuse me," Sky interrupts his conversation. "Here she is."

"Aight, yo. I'll get up with you later, man," he says to his friend. "Good looking out, shawty," he said as he turns to Sky. "And don't worry, she gonna be 'aight with me."

By T. Styles   63

"No problem, boy. Just do my friend right," Sky says as she switches away.

I'm alone with him and nervous. I ain't the go-hard bitch I use to be and, tonight, I don't feel like no shit. All I want to do is have a nice time and pretend that all the stuff going on in my life ain't. I don't want him calling me a whore or asking me how much I charge, like they usually do when they learn I trick. Men love breaking me down in public. They love reminding me of my position. But to prevent spoiled ass Sky from being upset, I decide to meet him anyway.

He's tall, attractive and dressed real fly. His mocha-colored skin doesn't have a mark on it, and the five o'clock shadow does him right. He's killing the leather blazer with the cap and Timbs. He has that Usher style going on real tough so before he say a word, I know he's my kinda nigga.

"Damn, I was wondering when you was coming over here, yo. I asked your friend about you a long time ago."

"Well, why you ain't come over to meet me yourself?" I ask, seeing if he's playing games.

"'Cuz I ain't know if your dude was here, yo. I got beef with niggas already 'cuz of dumb shit," he responds.

"Where you from?" The accent sounds like New York or B-more, but for real I ain't sure.

"B-more. Why?"

"Just asking. So what you want with me?" I say, hoping he doesn't want to know my prices. "And, be real 'cuz I ain't got time for no games."

"Yo, I'm just trynna check you...get to know you...see what's up...That kinda thing. Why? Your man in here or something?"

"Naw. I ain't got one of those. Why you keep asking?"

"'Cuz I told you niggas trip hard over bitches—I mean girls," he says.

"Well, I don't have a man right now," I reply as if I'd have one in the near future. This left me a little room in case I find out he is stupid and I don't want to be bothered. If he thinks I have a man, I can always come back to this moment.

"Well look, since you ain't ask and it took you forever to come over here, I'll tell you myself. I ain't got nobody I fuck with either, but I'm trying to get to know you."

"I was gonna ask you if you had somebody." I laugh.

"When, shawty? You got me working overtime here," he says as he *play* hit me. "What a nigga gotta do to get your attention?"

"You did it already," I respond, feeling happy I walked over here after all. "Well, where you live?"

"I just got a house over there by the Manor and I'm looking for somebody to kick it with from time to time. It could be you," he says, "if you want it to be."

"Oh, for real." I smile. "Well, we'll see. I need to make sure you ain't no stalker or nothing first."

"Naw…if you don't want me, I'll leave you alone." He smiles.

I believed him too.

"Who you be with?"

See, if he rolls with a certain crew then it ain't no use of getting to know him because they'd tell him I'm a hoe. They'll probably tell him anyway but if I get to spend time with him for a while and he starts to like me, maybe he won't care.

"I hang with a wrack of Baltimore cats. You probably don't know 'em."

"Oh," I say, feeling a little relieved because where I live is a long way from Baltimore. "Who you here with?" I need to eliminate Silver and them with the quickness, because nice or not, I'm not fucking with nobody they associate with.

"A friend of mine told me about this spot so, I had to check it out. Now, it's my turn to start asking some questions. Yo, why you single? You got a lot of kids or something?"

"No! I don't have any kids. I'm just doing me right now."

Black and Ugly

"Well not for long," he says as he grabs my hand. My pussy jumps and I want him right there.

"What you sipping on?" he questions.

"My girl Parade got us Incredible Hulks earlier."

"Awwww shit, shawty. You going hard. Well, since it look like that joint is almost empty, let me get you another one."

He flags some dude over and tells him to bring two drinks, Hypnotic mixed with Hennessy and, within five minutes, we're sipping together. I'm feeling bad for Parade 'cuz, at this point, I have been over here for about 30 minutes. I am pretty sure Sky didn't come back to keep her company, especially after their argument. I look over in the spot we were and she's gone. I haven't seen Sky in about 25 minutes, when she kept smiling because I was still talking to him. For all I know, Parade has met somebody because she looks real cute tonight.

"So what you do for a living, shawty?"

That hurts. I don't know what to tell him, because anything outside of saying "I'm a prostitute" would be a lie.

"I'm a consultant."

"A businesswoman. I like that shit," he responds as he wraps his arm around my waist and pulls me to him. "I can bring you home to Mamma. That's what's up."

There are a few dudes in here I've been with before that keep looking in our direction. I'm determined to stay until every last one of them leave even if it means me getting another ride. I don't want none of them clowns dropping the 411 on me behind my back. I want this one for keeps.

I am so glad that he doesn't know anybody around the way that I don't know what to do. There is finally a possibility that somebody is feeling me, and I don't want to mess it up. I'm being given a chance, a clean slate. I'm already forming in my mind that if God lets me keep him, I'd work for six more months, save up enough money and get a real job.

"I got good feelings 'bout you, shawty," he says as he smiles with all teeth in place. "So who you stay with?"

"By myself."

"Word? That's what's up. Look, write your number down so I can get up with you later."

See, he's fine, so he's getting the home and cell number. And I don't give nobody my home number but my friends. Just as I hand him my numbers, Parade comes running up to me holding Sky by the arm.

"We gotta get out of here! Where's Miss Wayne?" Parade asks.

She's nervous and jittery, and Sky looks out of it too. I glance down at Sky's white pants and see blood all over them.

"You alright, yo?" he asks Sky.

Sky nods up and down. Right then, I realize I don't know his name. I'm worried about my friends but not that much, 'cuz Sky gets into shit all the time. I figure she got into a fight and, once again, Parade bailed her out.

"I'ma walk her to the car," Parade continues. "Find Miss Wayne and let's get out of here! Hurry up, Daffany," Parade says as she runs behind Sky.

"Look, I have to go. What's your name?"

"Ed. Go see about your girl," he says in a concerned tone. "I'll get at you later. Do what you gotta do."

"Okay." I smile as I give him a hug and inhale his leather jacket.

As I leave him, I see a blueberry top approaching me, and I know it is Miss Wayne. He has his hand purse clutched real close and looks extra dramatic. I look around, notice people seem to be huddled in groups and then I realize something definitely went down. Once again, Silver's boys ruined a party. I think.

"Gurl, where Miss Parade and Miss Sky?" Miss Wayne yells.

"They went to the car. What the fuck is going on? Why is everybody gathered in groups?" I ask, realizing he knows more than I do.

"Somebody got stabbed. Let's get out of here. I'm not sure if I got a warrant out on me for those traffic tickets I ain't pay when I had Miss Rick's car, chile."

Right as he says that, the music stops and niggas are running out the front door. We make a beeline for the exit too and, almost, get out with no problem until Miss Wayne yells, "Aaaaggghhh!"

"What? What?"

"Bitch, I broke my new heel."

"You what?" I ask. "Boy, come on. Let's get the fuck outta here."

"Shit," he continues, picking up his size 13 and hobbling out the door.

The car ride is quiet on the way home. I'm scared when I think that either Parade or Sky had something to do with what happened. After all, why does Sky have blood all over her pants? Before that shit happened, my night was turning out nice for a change. I met a guy who didn't treat me like a whore and who

Black and Ugly

seemed to be really interested in me. And Sky, with her bullshit, ruined it again.

I come through my apartment door and reach in my purse for an E-pill and down it with water. I feel rattled with all the different emotions I have going on inside me. I plan to call Parade to get all the details first thing in the morning.

My phone rings.

Can it be him calling me already? I throw my drink down and run toward my junky bedroom to find the cordless phone. I can't find it. I hear the third ring but still can't locate it. Shit. I look under my bed and lift my pajamas off the floor. It's lying right there. I really do need to clean this room. I press the button before whoever it is hangs up.

"Hello," I say, out of breath.

"Is Daff in? It's Ed."

So, you know I'm sised, right? I just met him and already he's hitting me up. He didn't want Sky or anybody else; he wants me. He's probably calling to make sure I'm okay. After all, the way I left the party was fucked up.

"It's me," I say, smiling through the phone.

"You okay, yo?"

"I'm good, Ed. Thanks for calling me."

"It ain't no problem, shawty," he responds. "But look...my boy just told me you give the bomb ass head. How much you charge?"

I hang up the phone and cry myself to sleep.

CHAPTER 5

SMOKES

Smokes is taking it hard since finding out his wife was murdered. He can't believe someone had enough nerve to actually kill her, knowing full well what he'd do to them. He is the largest dealer in Hyattsville, Maryland, with over six shops around the surrounding areas. All he wants is to handle the funeral proceedings, bury his wife and find out who ruined his family.

"Sir, is there anything else I can do for you?" asks the officer who, just a few minutes earlier, told him the news of the murder.

"Naw. Ain't shit you can do for me," he responds, having no trust in the authorities. "I'll take it from here."

"Take it from here?" the officer questions. "I hope you don't intend on taking matters into your own hands, sir. Let us handle this."

"Yolanda," Smokes calls his maid, "show the officer the door."

The officers leave and Smokes summons the caretaker to soothe his son, who has been crying for his mother all morning. She takes the baby, kicking and screaming, to his room. Smokes, then, calls Silver to see if he has any information on what happened to his wife at the party.

"Silver, you know anything 'bout this?" he interrogates, without even announcing himself.

"Naw, man, but I'll do everything I can to find out. Just give me a few days."

"You got two," Smokes commands before hanging up the phone.

Smokes doesn't have time to cry. And even if he did, he doesn't like showing emotions, even when alone. But in his mind, whoever murdered his wife killed the only woman he'd ever love. There was no way on earth he could be able to sit around and pray the authorities caught the perpetrators. He decides to solve the mystery the old-fashioned way.

CHAPTER 6

PARADE

I wake up to the nagging ass voice of my mother at 9:36 in the morning. If she ain't yelling 'bout something stupid, she's yelling 'bout something dumb.

"Parade, get your black ass up and clean that fucking kitchen. You ain't gonna lay your funky ass around here all day and not do shit."

I jump up and lock the door before she comes barging into my room. I still need time to regroup from the craziest night of my life, and the last thing I want to see is her face. Thinking back on how much blood was around that girl's body, I'm sure she has to be dead or hurt really bad.

The phone rings, I hurry up and grab it. I know it's for me because no one calls my lonely ass mother…not even her own husband. If I don't grab it, she'll do her best job of attempting to embarrass me on the phone.

"Hello," I whisper after noticing its Miss Wayne.

"Hey, Miss Parade." His voice is so thick it sounds like his breath stinks. The mornings are the only times I remember he is still a man. "You okay, chile?"

"I'm fine, Miss Wayne. I'm just getting up, and my mother already yelling like she lost her fucking mind."

My mother yells before he responds, "Bitch, get your black ass off my phone. How dare you talk about me like that, you ungrateful little bitch."

"*Ooooh.* Bye, guurl," Miss Wayne says as he hangs up.

That's all I need. She's gonna be screaming in my face for the next 30 minutes until it is time for her to go to work, unless I get out this house. I grab my bag and stuff some undies and something to throw on in it. I decide to shower over whoever's house I crash at later. I slide on my shoes and decide that I'm on my way to Sky's. She lives in the building behind mine and we have a lot to talk about, anyway.

I open my bedroom door and my mother is in my face, just as I figured she would be.

"You've gotten too fucking disrespectful, Parade. I wonder if *Miss* Wayne," she says sarcastically, "talks to his mother like you talk to yours?" She's still tripping over the name he asked us to call him when he was in the fourth grade.

"Ma, look how you talk to me. You, or Daddy, never say nothing nice to me. The only thing you say is how black and ugly I am and he says nothing at all. I don't need to hear all that," I continue as I move toward the door.

Black and Ugly

Why couldn't I just leave without saying something to her? Now, she'll be all on my case and probably carry our business out into the hallway.

"I call you ugly 'cuz you are. And if you'd go out and get a job, you won't have to worry about me being in your face."

Remember, I said I knew I was ugly the moment she handed me a mirror? That's because she reminded me everyday from that moment forward. But, outside of her being 5'3", we look just alike. Maybe Grandma told her the same thing when she was growing up. I do remember her telling Daddy that Grandma did things like make her wear the same clothes three days in a row, when she was in high school, and about the time she forbade her to take a bath for a whole week.

"Ma, every time I get a job I get fired 'cuz you keep calling me telling me to come home and wash the dishes or cook Daddy something to eat. Them supervisors don't want to hear nothing 'bout me leaving work to fry my father some chicken. They have businesses to run."

"And there's something wrong with cooking dinner for your father? Wait till I tell him how you really feel. See, he thinks I'm too rough on you. But wait until he hears that you don't like cooking for him, that you complaining and shit."

"Ma, I didn't say that. I'm saying it's hard to keep a job when you do things like that. And the last time I said I couldn't leave work, you threatened to throw my things out."

"Don't try to get out of it now, Parade. If you feel that way, that's how you feel. But, I'll be making sure he knows."

I know what she's doing. She knows Daddy and me have a closer relationship than she and I have, even though it isn't perfect. The truth is it's hard to have one with him since he is hardly ever here. He's a construction worker who gets up early in the morning and comes back late at night. I know he's home when I smell his feet. He's always had terrible feet odor and use to leave his work boots directly outside of the door in the hallway. At first, the neighbors complained about how funky the hallway smelled but, eventually, they got over it but, when they were gone one day, he started leaving them in front of the door inside the apartment.

"You know what? Tell Daddy whatever you want, Ma. I'm outta here," I snap as I slam the door.

Once in the hallway, I rush out of the building so she can't see which one of my friend's houses I am headed toward. That's the only messed up part about living in the same complex as my friends. She knows where they live, especially Miss Wayne because he

Black and Ugly

lives in the same building as me. So, going to see him is definitely not an option.

I get outside and I see Melvin's car next to Daffany's building. His friend lives upstairs from her so I figure he's over there checking him out, but I am not in the mood to see him right now either.

I make it to Sky's building and I see Jay's car parked out front. I should turn around, but in a way, I want to see him. He called my phone over six times when I was at the party last night, and I wonder if it's possible for him to actually miss me.

"Hey, Sky. We need to talk," I tell her as she opens the door.

"I know. Look, come in and go to my room. I'm a get rid of Jay in a minute."

I walk in I see him eating pancakes at the kitchen table. Her parents' car isn't out front but, even if it was, they like Jay so much that he's there most of the time anyway. Unlike me, if I'm having company, the entire house has to be clear.

A strange feeling comes over me when I see him, and I'm kinda jealous at the scene. Just yesterday, he was blowing my phone up and now he's eating pancakes and bacon at her kitchen table.

"Hey, Jay," I speak as I walk toward Sky's room. He doesn't say anything to me, just nods.

"Parade, go in the room and I'll be there in a sec," she says, irritated by me acknowledging her man.

On the sneak tip, I look through her hamper to find the white pants. I find them and my heart sinks. Almost the entire front is covered in dried blood. I grab the pants and stuff them in my backpack before she comes into the room. I don't know why I did it. I just did. She spends 30 minutes with Jay before I hear the front door close.

She walks in the room, shaken up and real nervous.

"You hear anything yet?" she asks, closing the door as if we are not alone. "They know it was me?" she questions, sitting on the end of her bed.

"Calm down, Sky," I say, trying to relax her. She has me on edge, and I hadn't even heard anything. "No. I came by to see if you heard something," I continue as I get up and sit on the chair across from Sky so I can look in her face.

"Nothing, Parade. I'm so fucking scared I don't know what to do. Jay came over here last night but I didn't want to even see him."

"Oh…I didn't know he came over," I say, trying to prevent the jealousy from consuming me.

Black and Ugly

"Yes, but I didn't tell him nothing. I just hope she's okay. I ain't mean to hurt her, Parade, but she jumped in my face. You know I don't play that shit."

"Well what exactly happened?" I ask, feeling relieved that I will finally get the full story.

Sky takes a deep breath, and tears roll down her face. It's the first time I have ever seen her cry.

"She walked up to me and said, 'I know I know you from somewhere,' when I was outside hitting the last of the bob we had in the car."

"Where was Jewel?" I ask, attempting to bring light to the fact that the bitch left her alone.

"She was talking to Silver somewhere."

"Oh," I say as I shake my head. "I don't see why she would leave you by yourself. That's stupid."

"Later for that, Parade," she asserts, brushing me off. She knows what I am getting at though. "So anyway, she comes up to me and starts talking shit. I started to come get ya'll, but I ain't want her thinking I couldn't hold my own. We exchanged a few words and out of nowhere, she stole me. And when she did, she knocked me up against Donna's father's toolbox. My back still hurts now," she says as she stands up so I can see the black and blue marks on her back.

She sits down and says, "So once I was down, she started hitting me again with some long iron thing she found in the backyard. I still don't know where she got it from, Parade. I was yelling for her to stop, hoping somebody would come outside. But nobody could hear shit in the house over the music. And if you looked outside from the sliding glass door, it was too dark to see because there was barely any light. So, I had to defend myself, Parade. I fucking had to.

"I went in my purse and pulled out my knife and stabbed her in the stomach. I ain't want to go too deep, just deep enough for her to stop hitting me with that iron thing. But she fell down and started crying for help. I just got the hell out of there, and that's when you came outside and saw me. How did you know I was there?"

"I didn't," I answer as I take a deep breath to absorb her explanation. "I always look for you when we go somewhere. I know somebody's always fucking with you, and I wanted to have your back."

"Thanks, Parade. But you know who she was, right?"

"No...who was she?" I ask real nervously.

"It was the girl you fought at the mall. She was mad at the way you stomped her out that day, and she took it out on me."

"What?" I yell, standing. "The girl in the mall that day was the same one outside last night?"

She nods.

Shit! Shit! Shit! This was my fault. Sky could've possibly committed a murder, and it's all my fault.

"I'm so sorry, Sky," I say, hugging her. "I shoulda been there."

"It's cool. We have to do whatever we have to do to protect each other," she says. "I hope you got my back."

"You know I do," I respond, taking my place back in my seat. "Whatever you need me to do, I'll do."

I can't get over the fact that Sky really stabbed somebody, and it's so unbelievable because we just saw them girls the other day in the mall. Again, I try to imagine Sky lying down on the ground. She's right. It was too dark outside to see much of anything. But, I did see blood all over Sky's pants and the girl lying down with her hair partially covering her face. I also remember that she wasn't moving or crying for help. In fact, she was extremely still.

"I'm sorry 'bout all of this," I repeat. "I shoulda been there."

"It's too late for that right now. We gotta stay tight. But, you think she okay, Parade? You think she'll be fine?"

"Yeah...I think she's okay. But if she's not, nobody knows you were out there and it was a lot of people at that party."

"Not to scare you, Parade," she cries as her chest moves up and down, "but I hope she's dead. I really do. Because if she's alive, she *will* be able to ID me," she pauses, "and you too. I just know it."

I couldn't believe what she is saying but I know she's right.

"If she is dead, they'll probably put everything on Silver and them anyway. They always getting arrested. But if she ain't dead, we run the risk of her telling the cops."

"So in a way it's better if she's dead, right?" she reasons.

I can't nod, but it is exactly what I'm thinking.

"You ain't gonna tell nobody, right? I mean, Miss Wayne and Daffany don't know, do they?"

"I'm not telling nobody, Sky. Trust me. I promise. The less people who know, the better."

"That's what I'm saying. The less they know, the better."

She runs up to me and hugs me again. I had known her since elementary school and she never voluntarily laid her hands on me. It was always me, wanting and needing her friendship.

As she is hugging me, my cell phone rings. She wipes the tears from her face and says, "Who is it?" As if whoever is on the phone has information about what happened at the party.

Black and Ugly

"Who is it, Parade?" she asks again. "Answer the phone. They may be calling to tell you something about last night."

But I can't because the person, on the phone, just left her house.

CHAPTER 7

JAY

Jay is angry at Parade for not answering his calls. He feels that even though he's with Sky, Parade should be at his beck and call. He likes the idea of being able to control her and don't want her getting too far away from him. He is sitting in his car on his way to New York to re-up when he decides to call her again. The moment she answers the phone, he goes in on her.

"Where you at?" he asks her in a serious tone.

"I'm on my way to Miss Wayne's house. You know I was still over Sky's when you called me earlier, don't you?"

"Man, that girl ain't thinking 'bout us. She wouldn't even think I'd look your way. Trust me. So there's nothing to worry about."

He knows that hurt Parade, but he wants to be real with her. As far as he's concerned, Parade is somebody he fucks, and it's as simple as that. But, what he doesn't realize is that Parade gives him much more. Her kind ways, slowly but surely, are starting to make him fall for her and begin to hate the relationship he has with Sky even more. But, because he grew up in a household that looked down upon dark-skin women, he knows he can never put one on his arm, especially one that would be his ex-girl's friend.

"Oh," she says in a low voice. "I guess you're right. So what's up? Is something wrong?"

"Naw. I'm trying to fuck when I get back tomorrow," he declares.

"Where you going?"

"Why?" he yells.

"I was just asking. 'Cuz I wanted to know what time to be in the house."

"Man, I'm going to New York. And you need to be waiting on me whenever the fuck I call."

"I know, Jay," she says softly. "I will."

"The fuck wrong with you? You beefing 'bout what I said?"

"No...it's just that my hair is messed up, and I want to find a job."

"So what, you asking me for money?"

"No."

"Look, I'ma give you $300 tomorrow, but don't think you gonna keep running my pockets."

"Thank you, Jay."

"Thank you shit," he says, cutting her off. "Make sure you got my pussy ready."

"Okay..." she responds, trying to end an embarrassing moment. "I'll talk to you tomorrow."

He hangs up without a response. He's on the Baltimore Washington Parkway and decides to call Sky. Unlike calling Parade, he doesn't look forward to speaking to her. He feels that lately she has become too high on herself. But, her attitude is half his fault and half her parents.' They spoil that girl so much that she expects other people to do things for her instead of appreciating whatever is given.

"Hey, Sky. What you doing?" he asks, although he really doesn't care.

"On my way to Miss Wayne's."

"Oh. Who you with?" He asks.

"I'm by myself, boy. Am I seeing you tonight?"

"Naw. I'm on my way to New York."

"So when was you gonna tell me?"

"I did but you was running your mouth with that bitch."

"Naw, I don't remember all that, Jay," she says. "But anyway, what's up with tomorrow?" she asks, hoping he'd have room for her then. "I miss you already."

"Maybe later on that night. I got a lot of work to do. Niggas been slipping on the block lately, so I have to put them youngins back in check."

"Okay, baby. Well, don't keep me waiting too long. You don't want nobody else getting your attention, now do you?"

"No, Sky," he says, hating how she constantly throws other men in his face. "But look, I'll get up with you later, 'aight. I was just calling to check up on you right quick."

"Okay." She smiles. "You love me, right?"

"You know I do."

"But I want to hear you say it, Jay. You never tell me anymore."

"I love you. You better now?"

"Kinda," she says, disappointed she doesn't get the response she wants. "Call me when you..."

He hangs up before she can finish then speeds down the parkway on his way to New York. He's wondering why Parade has been on his mind so much lately. He knows that it is just a matter of time before he cuts Sky off. But, what he doesn't know is what that could mean for him and Parade.

CHAPTER 8

DAFFANY

Melvin knocks on my door at least three times. I figure something is wrong and, even though I don't want to, I decide to let him in. I ain't expecting or looking forward to company after last night. All I want is to be left alone.

Melvin was my John way before Parade started messing with him so I am playing over and over in my head if it is possible for her to have this shit. I pray she doesn't, but really can't be sure. I mean, she ain't got no symptoms, but it ain't like I had symptoms either. I just went in for a checkup because my uncle died from it six months ago, and I wanted to make sure I was okay. And when I did, I discovered I was positive. Ain't that something?

"Melvin, it's not cool for you to be coming 'round here no more. You should keep checking with Parade yourself. Eventually, she'll talk to you."

"I did and she not accepting my calls," he says as he throws his short hands up in the air. He's sweating despite the air conditioner being on full blast. His black shirt has a visible sweat stain under his chin and the dandruff, from his hair, is pasted on it.

"Well, give her some time. She'll come around," I say, trying to end our conversation so I can go back to bed.

"Why is it so dark in here? You expecting company?"

"Melvin...it don't make a difference if I'm expecting company or not. Now, you know Parade lives across the parking lot. I don't want her popping up over here and seeing you in my apartment."

"She'll just think I'm over here seeing my man," he advises as he takes a seat. "Don't even worry about her."

"Melvin, please," I pause taking a deep breath, "just keep calling her. I am not mentally stable enough to be getting into ya'll's love life. I have problems of my own."

"I'm tired of kissing her ass," he continues, ignoring my last statement. "I've decided that I'm going to let her come to me for a change."

"Okay," I say, wondering why he is even over here if he feels that way.

"Look, why don't you give me some head real quick? I've been stressing really bad lately."

I can't stand Melvin's short, stubby ass. He pays good money, though, and that's the only reason I be bothered with him. But, after he started messing with Parade, I've been trying my best to leave him alone. There have been many times I've tried to steer her away from him and, every time I did, Parade found another reason to stay, loneliness being the main one.

"Naw, Melvin. This ain't cool. You gotta leave."

"I'll pay you $100 to do it right now. That's enough for a couple of E-pills and everything. I know you still popping."

Damn. I am kinda broke and I can use the money, but I wasn't feeling putting my friend at risk. Having HIV puts a lot of shit in perspective for me when it comes to my friends. We sleep with a lot of the same guys and I'm worried if they got it or not.

"You gotta go, Melvin," I demand as I walk toward the door and open it. "Things will work out for you."

"Open your hand," he says right before hitting the door. I do and he drops six pills in it. I press the door closed and lock it. "Now get on your knees."

I need those pills to relax and I need them bad. It ain't like I am gonna sleep with him. I'm just gonna blow him and that will be the end of it. I'm on my knees, taking it out while moving the four-inch-long pubic hairs aside. Placing his sweaty, funky dick between my lips, I tell myself that it will all be over in a minute. Melvin places his hands behind my head, forcing himself deeper and deeper into my mouth. It gets to a point where hair and limp dick is stuffed down my throat so I almost gag.

"Ahhhh...shit," he cries out as he suddenly becomes harder.

I feel him throbbing and know he is on the verge of busting. I want him to hurry up because a minute longer and I will be throwing up all over the place.

"Open...open wide, Daffany," he demands.

Reluctantly, I do as his cum gets all over my face and inside my nose. Getting up off the floor, I rush him out so I can be alone with myself. Getting tired of thinking about what I had done, I take three pills and wallow in misery.

"Uhn-ahn, bitch. Get up. You ain't sleeping all day today. I been calling your ass all morning."

"Miss Wayne, I'm not feeling well. I just want to lay in my bed with the blinds closed and go to sleep."

"And I want to meet and marry a handsome prince with 11 inches of stiff dick, but it don't mean I'm going do it."

"You are a mess." I laugh, sitting straight up in bed. I know there is no way he is letting me off the phone until he's ready. I am surprised I even answered it. "What happened last night? Did you hear anything yet?" I continue laughing at his last comment.

"No. Miss Parade was over to Miss Sky's house and they both stopped by real quick earlier, but I had company."

"Don't tell me you're fucking that little high school boy again."

"No, and he graduated already, so mind your ugly business."

"You a mess. You should be ashamed of yourself."

"Girl, I'm not ashamed if he ain't," he responds. "Anyway, when I called them back to see where they were, neither one of them answered their phones so I don't know what's going on."

"You see that blood all over Sky's pants?" I ask, trying to figure out if he is thinking the same thing that Sky possibly had something to do with it.

"Yes," he says in a real low voice. "I hated thinking 'bout it too. It was a little too weird for me. You know what I'm saying? I mean, a girl gets stabbed, and Miss Sky got blood all on her pants. For what? Either she had something to do with it, or that was the worse case of menstrual cycling I've ever seen in my life."

I burst out laughing.

"What? What's so funny?" he says.

He's always even funnier when he ain't trying to be.

"Later for them hoes," he responds. "Let me come over, girl. You've seemed out of it lately, and I'm starting to worry about you. They together, so it's only right that we shoot the shit too."

"I'm fine, Miss Wayne, but I really do want to be left alone today. I have a lot on my mind."

"I won't bother you," he responds. "I'll bring over my homemade spaghetti," he teases. "And you'll never know I'm there."

Although Miss Wayne is a man, he out cooks all of us any day of the week. But still, I really want to be by myself. Besides, the smell of Melvin is still all over me, and I'm fucked up about it. I appreciate what Miss Wayne is doing, but I'm not feeling up to talking or any company.

Since Ed built me up and broke me back down in a matter of hours, I'm in a bad mood. Why is it that when you wanna change, other people won't let you? I'm on the phone for three minutes with Miss Wayne trying to convince him to leave me be then I end the call and go fast asleep.

The banging on my door sounds like it could be the police for real until I hear Miss Wayne yelling, "Get up, bitch."

BANG, BANG, BANG.

"The mothafucking pep squad is here."

BANG, BANG, BANG.

"Open this got damn door."

BANG, BANG, BANG.

As I walk to the door, I want to cuss all of them out 'cuz when he says pep squad, I'm sure Parade and Sky is with him too. But if you know my friends, you'll know that cussing them out won't work.

"Yes," I say as I open the door.

"Hey, girl. You okay?" Parade asks as she hugs me with her hair still in place and looking cute.

This is different because Parade is hard on hairstyles. She never knows how to keep them for too long. They didn't last on me either, that's why I always rock ponytails.

"Damn, bitch. Turn some lights on in here," Sky says as she opens up all my blinds.

I close the door and tie my robe.

"Damn," they all say when the light reveals my filthy apartment. I'm lightweight ashamed.

"Do you ever clean up, girl?" Sky asks. "You ain't pregnant, are you? I ain't ready to be no god mommy."

"And just what make you think you would be the god mommy, bitch?" Miss Wayne says as he jumps in her face, with his plum-smuggling jeans on.

"And what makes either of you think you would be the god mommy?" Parade proclaims as she pushes both of them. "'Cuz Daffany knows I'm the only one with good enough sense to take care of the baby. Tell 'em, Daffany," Parade says as she looks at me. "Tell them who'd be the god mommy. It's only right they should know now anyway."

"Well luckily for my unborn child, I'm *not* pregnant." I smile at my friends who were going back and forth in front of me. "Now I'm feeling what you guys are doing but I really want to be left alone. Please."

"How did things go with that guy last night?" Sky asks. "He came over to see you? That's why you tired?"

"No," I respond as I start to cry.

"What's wrong?" Parade inquires as she runs over to me. "What happened?"

"Let's just say it's true, you can't make a whore your housewife. My own words make me sick to my stomach.

"Fuck that mothafucka. He better recognize that most housewives are whores anyway, chile. They fuck, suck and do anything else they can so these mens would take care of 'em." He continues, glancing at Parade. You ain't no different. You just ask for yours up front."

In a crazy way, he has a point.

"I feel you, Miss Wayne, but I'll really like to be alone right now."

I hate seeing the looks on their faces, but they'll be worse if I attempt to entertain them because although I don't want to admit it, Ed really fucked me up, and it's hard to shake the feeling of not being wanted. When people already know I trick and say it, I'm not fazed because it is what it is. But, he believed I was a businesswoman. He believed I was a woman just doing the damn thing while somebody, knowing about my past, hated on me. Maybe, I should just be who the fuck I am and stop worrying about what people think.

"Look, go in there for now and go to sleep. Let us take care of everything out here. And leave the door open too," Miss Wayne continues, breaking me out of my thoughts. "We wanna get in there next." He pushes me toward my bedroom.

Black and Ugly

"No, serious guys," I say as I walk out. "I really want to be left alone."

"Bitch, get in that damn room," Sky yells. "We got this shit under control, and you gonna thank us for it later too."

"Yeah get in the room, *whore*." Miss Wayne laughs.

He's trying to bring light to something he knows is bothering me. But, hearing the words leaving his mouth still hurt. I walk into my room then lie on my bed feeling bad about sleeping while they clean my house and for being bad company. But, the sounds of them moving around helps me go to sleep because I know they care about me, no matter what.

CHAPTER 9

SKY

The news has everybody stuck. I wish I never turned on the TV, but it wouldn't change shit. First, we were playing Taboo after cleaning Daffany's apartment, now we are watching the results of a crime that I committed. Coming back into the living room I hear:

"Sources are calling this a robbery gone bad. Apparently, the suspect attempted to rob the victim but killed her when she refused to comply. Sources, also, say Melony Parker was an active member of society, having contributed to over six charities in the Washington, DC area by donating funds and volunteering her time. She is mourned by her husband and infant son, Chandler.

I abruptly turn the TV off before they see or hear more.

"Why you do that?" they all scream.

"'Cuz we were playing a game, so let's play it."

"But we were looking at that," Miss Wayne says.

"I want to play the game," I whine, taking my original place on the couch. "We can watch TV at home."

"I didn't know it was so serious," Daffany responds, remaining on the subject. "I wonder what happened," she continues as she looks over at me.

I know she's wondering if I had anything to do with it. And since she knows I don't go for disrespect, she's probably sure I had everything to do with it. But I ain't saying or admitting to shit. And Parade better not either.

"I don't know but all I got to say is if she was so nice, she wouldn't't've been at Donna's party. Everybody knows what pops off at her things," I observe.

"What does that say about us?" Daffany asks. "We went too."

"You know what I mean."

"No, I don't. So what…she deserved to be killed?" Miss Wayne probes as he clutches the top of his shirt. "Please tell me you're not that cold, Miss Sky."

"Wayne, stop being a drama queen. All I'm saying is that the media lies, and that people are soooo fake. Why is it that when a person's alive he gets on everybody's nerves but when he dies, he will be sorely missed? It's bullshit," I yell.

"Did you know her, Sky, or are you saying it was okay for her to die? Because I don't understand what your point is," Daffany interrogates.

"I'm not saying that it was okay for her to die, Daffany. Stop putting words in my mouth. I'm not saying shit about her deserving to die. I just know the media loves to make someone look like Mother Theresa when they're dead, instead of what they were really like. The media should be honest. If she donated to the Red Cross one day and gave head the next, tell the full story. No offense, Daffany."

"And none taken, bitch."

"When I die, tell the truth," I continue.

"Don't worry, honey. We'll make sure everybody knows what an evil bitch you were. That will definitely be taken care of," he adds.

"Good, just as long as it's the truth, I ain't got shit to say about it."

"You won't have shit to say about it anyway, baby, 'cuz you'll be dust," Miss Wayne says as he pokes his lips out.

"Everybody needs to calm down," Parade interrupts. "A lot of shit has happened, and we shouldn't let that ruin our friendship just because we were there. Now I feel bad about what happened to her, too, but we can't get into a fight fest with each other 'bout it either."

"Miss Parade is right. Guurrl, when you start telling us what to do? I kinda like that shit though.

Command us, honey," he says as he reaches over and hit her on the leg.

Parade may have said that shit, but I ain't buying her little friendship comment. I'm just hoping she can keep my secret. Still, I haven't got around to finding out if she's really into Jay. Honestly, I don't want to give her the satisfaction of thinking I really consider her an option. But if I find out she's fucking Jay, I'll be stabbing her ass next.

"I just hope that whoever that mothafucka is gets exactly what's coming to them. It's because of that bastard that her baby don't have a mother anymore. That's tragic," Miss Wayne says.

What the fuck is he talking about? As usual he is making a scene and being over dramatic. Her baby probably didn't even know her fucking ass.

"I agree, Miss Wayne. Whoever the bitch is who killed that girl deserves to fucking die," Daffany says as she looks at me again.

I know she's talking 'bout me. And, since she wants it that way, I decide I don't need to be around them. I know one thing; I could have been doing something else besides cleaning her funky-ass apartment.

"Well I'm outta here," I state as I stand and grab my purse.

"Why, Sky? We were having a nice time before all this happened," Parade asks. "Let's talk. Don't leave like this."

"Yeah, we were having a blast," Daffany says all nonchalant and shit.

"Is that why you called me a bitch?"

Everybody is silent.

"That's what I thought. It's obvious that I've irritated everybody just as much as ya'll irritated me, so let me go somewhere where I'm wanted – home."

"Good night, Miss Thang," Miss Wayne chimes in.

"Good night, Wayne," I retort, deleting the Miss that I know he loves.

I'm on my way out the door and I get angrier. Since Parade is so concerned with friendship, I wonder if she knows what it means. I give that dirty black bitch everything - clothes and money when we hang out - but my man is off limits.

"Parade, can I use your cell phone? I want to call Jay real quick," I ask, looking for specifics to see if she has really been with him.

"Ummm, you can use my phone, Miss Sky. And Miss Daffany's phone is working too," Miss Wayne jumps in.

"No...I want to use Parade's phone. Daffany doesn't like her number being given out, and he might not recognize yours because I've never used it before, so hand me your cell phone, Parade," I demand.

"You know you can use my phone, Sky. Stop being a bitch," Daffany responds. "It's not a fucking problem. You act so spoiled when you can't have your way."

"No thank you, honey. I'd rather walk up the block to the store on the corner than to use your precious phone."

"Isn't that odd, since your apartment building is right behind mine? Somehow that corner comment makes you sound really stupid, doesn't it?" Daffany says.

"Fuck you, Daffany. I want to use Parade's phone because I've used it before, and he'll answer it if he recognizes the number."

"Well, the girl doesn't want you to use it so stop making a big deal and use mine instead," Miss Wayne says.

"Wayne, shut the fuck up and let Parade talk. Parade, can I please use your phone?"

"Uh...my battery's dead, Sky. You really should use Miss Wayne's. I'm sure Jay'll answer it even if he don't recognize the number," she utters as she begins to sweat and stutter.

"So what? You telling me about my man now, Parade? How would you know any fucking thing about my man?"

"I don't, Sky. Where is this coming from? I didn't do anything to you," Parade replies.

"Look, say yes or no. All that other shit you talking is bullshit."

"I'm sorry, Sky. Please don't be mad, but I'll have to say no."

"You a sneaky bitch! I'm not fucking with you no more, Parade. I better not find out that you fucking with me either," I say as I run out the door, not wanting to alert anybody else that I am worried about her taking my man.

I walk to my building with my suspicions confirmed that something must be going on between Jay and Parade. But, what I didn't understand is how? He hates dark-skin girls and Parade ain't even attractive. However, I never expected Miss Wayne to be in on it too.

Suddenly, the cool air takes over me and I realize I left my jacket, but I ain't going back into that apartment. My friends have stabbed me in the back, and I don't want anything else to do with them.

I try my hardest not to cry but as I turn the corner, I can't hold back my tears.

CHAPTER 10

SMOKES

"Don't worry 'bout Quincy Manor. Everything's cool," Silver says on the phone. "Just do you, and if there's anything you need, I don't even give a fuck, I'm down with it. You know I got your back. No problem."

Smokes is silent. He's pondering whether he can count on Silver to handle the business around the way, let alone anything pertaining to his wife. Thinking more about it, he realizes that dealing with Silver, on the level where things need to be done and done right, is not a good idea.

"What I need can't nobody give me. And that's my mothafucking wife back. Can you do that?"

Silence.

"Exactly. So what you saying right now, I'm not trying to hear."

"I can't bring Melony back, man, but I can give you the bitches who had something to do with it. That should take care of a lot of the problems for you, right?"

"Not really," Smokes answers, being more difficult than he originally intended when their conversation first started.

"What you mean?" Silver asks.

"I mean somebody took my fucking wife away, so killing a mothafucka ain't gonna fix the bigger problem."

"I know, man," Silver says, sensing there is nothing he can say that will help the situation.

"Naw, you don't know, youngin'. Don't tell me you know 'cuz you ain't got a kid, and you don't know what the fuck it feels like to have his mother gone."

"I feel you, man."

"Oh, you do?" Smokes responds sarcastically. "Do you know how fucked up shit is when a kid grows up without his mother? I want 'em to suffer, Silver. I want whoever did this brought to me and tortured. I don't want no fucking mistakes." He pauses to allow the severity of his desires to sink into Silver's consciousness. "Now what's the information you have for me?"

"Well, we found out that three bitches and a faggy left the party real quick. My mans said they got the fuck out of dodge."

"Everybody was leaving that mothafucka. How you know they had something to do with it?"

"My mans says Sky, Jay's bitch, had blood all over her pants. I think at the very least, she knows who did it, if she ain't do it herself."

Smokes can't believe what he heard. He doesn't know Sky personally, but he knew exactly who she is. He fails to understand why she would want to kill his wife. He does know she's a spoiled little bitch and that's the extent of his familiarity.

"Something ain't right with that. I don't want no guessing with this situation, man. I need to know for sure that she did it. No guessing! I wanna know that the money I put on whoever's head is money well spent."

"You got it," Silver says, getting excited about possibly getting put on. He knows Smokes pays good money for slinging in the hood, so a hit will be worth way more.

"Now give me the number of that nigga from Texas you use," Smokes commands as he quiets his baby.

"You hear this shit, right?" Smokes interrupts before he can get the info. "My son's been crying nonstop since his mother didn't come home. Yeah...Yeah...I need this shit handled."

"I don't know 'bout using Eclipse, man. I only use him for out-of-town jobs. I do everything else myself," Silver insists, trying to hint around that he's more than capable for the job. "Plus, Eclipse's real expensive, and he moves too slow. He analyze too much shit for me instead of going in a mothafucka blazing."

"Well, that's what I need. Somebody to do the shit right."

"Well, I know some niggas that'll find them bitches and murder them tonight for half the price."

"Who you talking about? Your fucking family members?" Smokes asks, already knowing he's referring to his people.

"Naw," Silver replies, lying. "Uh...they do live in the Manor, so for real, it ain't nothing but a thing."

"No thank you, nigga. Mothafuckas are already looking at me and if they're from the Manor, that shit's too close for comfort. They sitting 'round waiting on me to do something now. All I need is the feds getting a hold of a local nigga and blow my spot up. I'll just stick with the out-of-town cat," Smokes persists with his mind made up.

"I'm telling you, Smokes. These niggas are..."

"Did you hear what the fuck I said, man?" he interrupts. "My kid is growing up without his mother. I ain't trying to have him growing up without a father too." He yells so loudly, he wakes up the baby who went to sleep just minutes ago. "Rosa," Smokes yells, "come get Chandler and put him to sleep."

The nanny takes the baby and leaves out of the room then Smokes continues his conversation. "Like I

Black and Ugly

said, I want this shit done right. Every time I use you and your brother to take care of something the nigga next to him ends up dead. So…I'm not fucking with you or any of them other stupid-ass niggas you run with. Now I want you to get in contact with that dude, tell him the situation and have him call me back."

"You got it," Silver reluctantly responds.

"I'm out."

CHAPTER 11

MISS WAYNE

"Listen, chile, I don't fuck around when it comes to my money. And, I know you know this," I say in a high-pitched voice. "It would be ungood. Trust me, honey."

"Bitch, you always think somebody fucking with yo' shit. Now I got you everything you asked me to get and then some."

"I DIDN'T ASK FOR NO RUBBER DICKS, BITCH! So how you get me everything *I* asked for?"

"You said I could get something once I got what was on the list."

"I said you could get *something* when I got *everything* on the list. Now you tell me what's wrong with this picture."

"I did cover the list...damn. Why you acting like that?"

"Well how come I don't see the Dooney and Burke purses in the box? Where are those, bitch? I got mothafuckas looking for shit I ain't got," I yell with one hand on my hip. "I tell you what you're doing. You making me look bad."

"Oh, guuurll…aren't you blowing things a little out of proportion?" Miss Rick says. "I mean, every other time you asked for something, I got it. So what on earth are you talking about?"

"Oh, Bitch you are doing shows. I know you lost your mind. What about the Bratz?"

"What?" Miss Rick asks, confused.

"I said what about the Bratz doll, bitch?"

"I don't know. I don't watch that shit."

"You were supposed to get that Bratz bitch and bring her back to me. That woman was calling me asking me about that thing for weeks after her daughter's birthday. And what did you do? Forget all about the Bratz doll to get some edible thongs," I rant then pause for a moment to catch my breath. "So, don't tell me this is the first time."

"Okay, and that was the only thing I ever forgot," Miss Rick responds.

"It is not. Today you forgot the purses."

"I didn't forget. I couldn't find them wretched purses. You ain't getting no money for 'em no how, 'cuz ain't nobody carrying them ancient bags."

"Sweety, I got customers who ordered them purses. Everybody don't like the sequins purses you be carrying around. Some people got taste."

"Get over yourself, Miss Wayne."

"Now, I let you hold the credit card to get everything on the list and a few things for you once my list was cleared. What I'ma tell them hoes when they come see me and I ain't got their shit? Damn, Miss Rick."

"I'm sorry, girl. I can go back tomorrow," he pleads, finally realizing he's wrong.

"No you can't go back tomorrow. Once you use a card, it's done with. That's all we need is the heat from Judy because you going back using hot-ass credit cards. I'll get another one tomorrow." Shaking my head at the thought of the cops being after me for Miss Rick's stupidity.

"Okay. But when you gonna put me on so I can get my own customers?"

"When the fuck you do what I tell you to. That's when."

"Whatever, *pink* bitch."

"Look, girl, I gotta go, but next time I send you to get something, don't run to the counter to buy your toys before my list is complete. Now bye, chile."

He gets on my full and complete set of nerves. He knows I need the Dooney and Burke purses for them bitches. They gonna kill me. *Damn*, I think as I stomp my left foot. They've been hitting me up ever since I started back fucking with this credit card shit again. See, I had to chill out for a while. Somebody hated, and the police's narrow asses were all over me. That was about six months ago but, now, I'm back in business.

BANG, BANG, BANG.

Who the fuck is that? Oh my word, please don't tell me the cops saw that bitch bring this shit to my house.

BANG, BANG, BANG.

Oh no! I'm going to jail. Oh God, I can't go to jail. Please don't let me go to jail. Do you know what they'll do to me if I get locked up? Well, that won't be too bad but I still like to come and go as I please. I can visit, but I certainly don't want to make it my home.

And here I am sitting on over $25,000 worth of shit. I mean I got it all. Louis Vuitton, Gucci, Tiffany jewelry sets and La Perla undies - I mean everything. Calm down, girl. Sometimes, I get so worked up and, most of the time, it's for nothing. Let me look through the peephole first.

OH SHIT! It *is* Judy, CHILE.

God, let me get out of this here and I'm never doing this again. Let them leave me alone and I'm never touching another credit card in my life.

"Mr. Wayne Peterson, we know you're in there."

"One minute please. Just 'cuz I'm in here don't mean I ain't taking a shit."

"We'll wait."

I know they will. Greasy mothafuckas. I throw the goods in my bedroom and lock it with the deadbolts I had put on for added security. See, I've been robbed several times and them bastards will want my treasures the moment they find out I'm back in business. They don't wanna pay for shit around here.

So, I fixed their asses and had this special metal door put in with an alarm system and deadbolts. The rental office doesn't know shit about that door. If somebody breaks in the living room, they'll be short 'cuz the real shit is in my chest and I only fucks with out-of-town customers now. No more hood niggas for me.

"May I help you?" I ask as I open the door.

"Yes...we'd like to ask you some questions about the death of Melony Parker."

Whoa! That's a close call. I feel like offering them some bacon, eggs and cheese. I'm so happy. After all, I was there, but I ain't have nothing to do with what happened to that poor chile. So, I don't have anything to worry about. I mean... I do feel sorry for the young lady though.

"Sure, officers. Come in, please."

They flash their badges, walk in and sit down. They could've flashed two pictures of their bigheaded babies and I would've never known the difference. All I see is two men and I'm open.

"Thank you, sir," one of them says.

"Can I get you some coffee or something? Maybe some potato salad and chicken?" I ask them.

"No, sir. We just want to ask you some questions, that's all."

"Okay...shoot! Well...not literally, but I am ready and willing to be as cooperative as possible. You can count on me, officers," I tease as I sit down on my sofa and cross my legs.

See, it ain't even been five minutes and I already have their full attention. My silk short set from Vickie's kills 'em every time.

"I understand you were at the party, Mr. Peterson. The one that Donna Samone gave in Northeast, Washington, DC where Mrs. Parker was killed. What can you tell us about that night?"

"First off, call me Miss Wayne. Mr. Peterson is *so* formal."

They nod in agreement.

"I mean, it is important to be friendly, right?" I'm laying it on thick, but I want to loosen them up. They look so frustrated but, boy, are they edible like two sweet brown sugar daddies and I want to suck on and bite into both of 'em.

"Mr. Peterson, please answer our questions."

"Okay. No need to get all antsy. I am just being friendly."

"Well, that's not why we're here. We're here because the night of the party, a young woman was murdered, not to sit here and eat potato salad or play games with you."

As much as I want to dip my hand into a jar of Vaseline and slap the fuck out of him, he's right. I'm acting like a slut and they're here on business. It's just that. It's not often that I get two police in my house that ain't looking to arrest *me*. It's actually sort of refreshing, and I want to take advantage - or shall I say I want them to take advantage. You get the idea.

"I'm ready to cooperate, but I'm afraid I can't tell you much. Alls I really know is that I saw Miss Parade running toward the door with Miss Sky, and I knew something was up."

"Why, sir…I mean, Miss Wayne?" Officer D. Hurts says as he looks at his partner.

"Well 'cuz we had planned for that party all week, that's why," I explain as if the officer should've known. "We had these cute little shiny outfits on and everything. Well, maybe not shiny but real cute. And I know they would've never left so early if something wasn't wrong," I continue as I smack my lips.

I'm noticing that D. Hurts is looking at my fingers when I talk. See, I'm a typical girl so I can't say a word without moving them.

"Sooooo, the moment I saw them leaving and saw everybody else talking, I asked somebody what happened and I found out that someone was stabbed. Miss Daffany was talking to some guy so I grabbed her, and we went to find our friends."

"So who did you go with?"

"Miss Daffany, Miss Parade and Miss Sky."

"Can you tell us where to find them?"

"Yes. I can write their addresses down too. We all live in the same complex."

"Thank you. That'd be very helpful," Officer S. Oakley says.

"I try, honey."

I write down the addresses and they leave, so I am on my way to the phone to warn my girls that they are next on the list. Before I lock the door, good, Officer Hurts comes back to drop off his card. On the back is his cell number with the words *call me anytime.*

Now, I'm in a whole 'notha world.

CHAPTER 12

PARADE

I'm daydreaming about what happened with me, and my mother, last night when Carol comes over and checks my hair under the dryer.

"You almost done, girl. Now don't fuck up your hair this time 'cuz I almost couldn't squeeze you in," she says, placing the dryer on my head before walking off.

As I sit there, I think about my mother again and why she hates me so much.

Last Night

"Parade! Parade! Get the fuck up!"

Like always, I popped out of the bed to see what she wanted. When I saw her sorting out dirty clothes on the floor, I got on my knees to help. She told me the day before that we had to wash so I figured it was

Black and Ugly

time, but, the moment I grabbed a red shirt to place in the color pile she had already formed, she ran over to me with a pair of white filthy underwear in her hands.

"What is this? You nasty bitch!"

Before I could answer, I was knocked backwards, and my ankle felt like it had twisted underneath me.

"What did I do?" I asked as she continued to mush the seat of the shit-stained underwear in my face.

"What did you do?" she yelled, straddling me. "What did you do? I'll tell you what the fuck you did. You walk around here all day like your ass don't stink and expect me to clean up behind you. Look at this shit. I know you don't expect me to wash these."

"Ma," I said stealing a glimpse of the drawers in her hand, "those are not mine."

"Well whose are they? Because, they damn sure ain't mine," she continued steadily pressing the stain up against my lips.

"Ma, please," I said, finally able to get from underneath her, "can you listen to me for a second?" As I glanced at the underwear she dangled in her hand, I saw the size and knew immediately they were hers.

"No," she said, getting up. "I want you to wash all of the drawers in here by hand."

As she walked over to the pile of clothing, she shoved a bunch of dirty underwear in my arms. Some belonged to me but most of it was my mother and father's.

"But Ma…"

"Did you hear what the fuck I said, Parade?"

I nodded.

"Well do it now," she screamed in my face.

"Ma, I'm not doing that," I said as nicely as I could without getting her upset.

"Oh you not, are you?" she continued. "Well, you can get your shit and get the fuck out of my house."

She shoved me toward the door and pushed me out. When it closed, I broke down crying because I could not figure out why she hated me so much. With nothing on but my bra and some pink cotton shorts, I knew I couldn't stay out in the hallway like that forever. I knocked several times before she decided to open it.

"So what are you gonna do?" she asked as she opened the door with the chain still on.

"I'll wash 'em, Ma."

With that she removed the chain and let me in. When I got to the bathroom I could barely see because tears blurred my vision. My mother was starting to make me hate her and I knew if I didn't leave soon, I'd probably want to kill her or myself.

"Hurry up, Parade," she said, bringing the dishwashing liquid in the kitchen for me to use.

Black and Ugly

When I placed the clothes in the bathtub, she came right behind me turning on the shower instead of the faucet. I got soaked and the hairstyle, I worked so hard to keep, was ruined. I heard her laughing behind me as I jumped up trying to salvage it.

"Looks like your little hairdo got ruined," she said, smirking. "Oh well, it didn't look like shit anyway. Now, hurry up and do what the fuck I asked you to."

I spent the next hour hating her and myself.

"Oh my goodness," an old lady says as she sat next to me under the dryer. "You are beautiful."

"Who?" I question. "Me?"

"Yes." She smiles. "You remind me of my daughter."

I examine her vanilla-complexioned skin, trying to imagine how someone so light could have a daughter as dark as me.

"Thank you," I respond. "Carol does a really good job on my hair."

"Sweetheart, I can't see your hair," she replies. "I'm talking about your face. You're beautiful."

As I sit here and listen to her, I can't stop the tears from forming in my eyes. In my entire life, no one had ever called me pretty let alone beautiful. And here I am, speaking to a total stranger who has nothing to gain by complimenting me.

"I appreciate it but I don't think I'm nowhere as pretty as you are. I wish I had your complexion."

"Why do you say that?" she asks with her face distorted.

"Well I think light-skinned people are pretty. And, I'm far from light-skin."

"Sweetheart, I don't know who you've been talking to but beauty is skin deep. It doesn't matter if you're light or dark. If you're beautiful, you're beautiful. And if you haven't learned to appreciate your beauty, both inside and out, I beg you to start today."

"I'm ready for you, Ms. Skarlett," one of the hairdressers informs.

"Okay," she responds, looking away before turning back to me. "Remember, sweetheart, love yourself because if you don't nobody else will."

The dryer has gotten extremely hot and my ears are burning but I continue to sit here, wondering if what she said could possibly be true.

CHAPTER 13

PARADE

"What's going on, Sky?" I ask as I smooth the Proactiv mixture on my face, praying that it works.

Today, I woke up deciding to take better care of myself since nobody else cared and I figured I'd start with my face. I know Sky said she knew somebody who used it and it didn't work, but I decided to see for myself.

"What you doing, girl? And why the water sounds so close? You ain't taking no bath with me on the phone, are you?" she yells in my ear.

"No. Just washing my face. Let me rinse this stuff off real...."

"What stuff? You using that Proactiv shit? 'Cuz I told you it don't work."

"I know," I state, feeling disappointed due to her reminding me that it may not work. "But I just wanna see what happens. So what's up?" I ask, trying to rush her off the phone and finish what I'm doing since Jay is coming over.

"You hear anything yet?"

"Oh...'bout that?" I ask, not wanting to discuss it over the phone. "Maybe we should talk about this kind of thing in person, Sky. I think that would be better."

"No need. I just want to make sure you won't betray me since we was beefing the other day."

"I wasn't beefing with you. You were mad at me, Sky."

"It wasn't that I was mad. You've been acting funny, lately. Like you not being real with me, or something. And, the only reason I'm calling now is to make sure you'll keep our little secret. After all, this is your fault."

I sit on the toilet to let the toner work throughout my skin failing to understand why Sky is so dead set on making me feel bad about something I already feel guilty for. She's called me six times already saying the same thing. And each time, my answer was the same. I would never sell her out.

"I'll never betray you, Sky. I swear it. I told you that already," I assure her, hoping the truth can be heard in my voice.

"When you say you wouldn't betray me, does that mean with *everything*?"

Her words hit me like an electric shock. I wonder what she means, wondering if she knows about me, and Jay, after all. The only thing that allows me to brush it off is that I don't know Sky to bite her tongue for anything or anybody.

"What do you mean?" I ask, hoping she would clarify.

"You know what I mean. I need to know that you wouldn't stab me in the back after all the things I've done for you and I'm not just talking about with the girl, Parade. Because if I find out you're phony, I'm never fucking with you."

"I know," I say. "You don't have to worry about nothing. My lips are sealed."

"I hope so." She ends the call.

CHAPTER 14

MARKEE

"I ain't got nothing on me, I swear. Why you doing this? Please don't hurt me."

"Shut the fuck up, bitch, and open the door," Markee yells at an unsuspecting girl entering her apartment near Quincy Manor.

Markee took the hallway light out and was lying in the cut waiting for his unknown victim to come along. He was happy to see the young black girl, in her twenties, going into the apartment right in front of where he stood, hidden in the corner.

"Okay, okay. Please don't hurt me. Take what you want," she says as she opens the door and he follows her in.

Once inside, Markee feels relieved. Sometimes, he had gotten certain people who would rather take their chances with him, based on youthful looks and speech, than to give him their money. But, that doesn't do anything but make him more vicious over time. He won't hesitate to pull the trigger if somebody fails to give him what he wants.

"Where your money at?" he yells as he locks the door behind him while keeping the gun pointing in her direction.

"It's right here. This all I got," she pleads as she empties her purse.

"You ain't got nothing else here?" he asks as he motions for her to go to her bedroom and check in there. "I know your folks be balling."

Once in her bedroom, he finds a few pieces of cheap jewelry and an iPod. He quickly puts them in his pocket and motions for her to go back into the living room.

"You sure you ain't got nothing else in here?" he persists, feeling excited by the control.

"No, this all I got."

"Damn... Where's your ATM card? I know you got one."

"Yes. And if you want, we can get some money out tonight," she suggests, trying to take her chances back outside instead of in the apartment.

"Naw. Write your pin number down. And if it's not right, I'ma come back and finish you off. You don't want to fuck with me. You probably heard of me already anyway," he brags as he begins to feel himself by taking pride in the crimes he's committed around the neighborhood.

"I probably do." She smiles since she senses he wants recognition. "I'll write down my pin number for you."

"Good. 'Cuz I don't want to hurt you."

"Thank you," she says, appreciative that the possibility of living exists.

She writes the number down while he sits on the couch and tells her to come over to him. He admires how attractive she is, even though she's afraid. Her tight jeans fit her body like a pitcher's glove. And the waist-length jacket shows the thickness of her breasts. He sees she isn't moving then yells at her to come to him. This time, she does what she's told. To satisfy his sick, insatiable sexual needs, he makes her suck his dick. Not wanting to do anything but save her own life, she complies.

He takes a few pieces of mail, promises to finish her off if she ever said anything to anybody then leaves. With the ATM card in hand, he goes straight to the bank to take the maximum he can withdraw. Being young and naïve, he fails to realize that ATMs take pictures.

CHAPTER 15

PARADE

Sky's hairstylist Carol really laid my tracks. I've never felt attractive until now. I wasn't even thinking about long weave at first, but I'm glad she suggested it. For $250 though, this shit better last. Men have been beeping at me ever since I stepped out the shop. I even had a few girls ask me who did my hair, and that has never happened. I wonder if my mother will like it. I know my friends will, especially Miss Wayne and Daffany. I'm not sure about Sky, though. But for the first time in my entire life, I can hold my head up.

Miss Wayne was right regarding me saying something to Jay about giving me more money. I hate going somewhere with Sky paying for me, only to hear about it later, especially when we are fucking the same man. But ever since I talked to him about it a few days ago, he's been hooking me up. He still reminds me that he doesn't have to do shit for me but, at least, he's doing something.

He went from calling me a whore everyday to saying it once a week while all I could think' about was

Miss Wayne saying, "Don't no pussy grow on trees, including yours." It wasn't easy asking him at first, but I don't want to be embarrassed in public when I hang out with Sky and them anymore. Remembering that day in the car was enough for me to put my foot down with him.

"Parade, don't think you're cute just 'cuz you got that shit in your head. You ain't no better than nobody else. Trust me. Who paid for it anyway?"

"Why, Mamma?"

"'Cuz bills are due 'round here, that's why. And if you got money to pay for your hair, you got money to pitch in."

"Mamma, the bills were still gonna be due, even if I didn't get my hair done," I tell her as I walk toward my room, hoping and praying she won't follow me.

"Parade, nothing in here is free. You got to pay your way around here."

"With what, Mamma? I ain't got no job," I yell.

"With the same money you used to get your hair done. It was a waste of time anyway. It doesn't even look real."

"Okay, Mamma. Is that why you're mad?"

"Is that what you think, Parade?" she says as she put her hands on her hips. "Anybody can put some shit in their hair, darling. Why do you think it was so easy for you to do?"

"Mamma, why do you have to bring me down all the time? Why can't we get along? I love you but I wonder if you ever loved me."

I look in her eyes, searching for anything that would convince me that she did care about me, but I see nothing.

"Stop whining, Parade. You my child so I have to care about you."

"No you don't, Mamma. No, you don't *have* to care about me. And I'm starting to realize that's the case," I respond as I lay back in my bed with my feet on the floor while she continues to yell over my head.

"Parade, please. You just lazy and expect nobody to say nothing. That's all it is."

"Mamma...what is it really?" I ask as I sit up and look at her. "Do you want me to be sad all the time? 'Cuz I am. There's no need to try and make me feel worse. Do you want me to hate myself, Mamma? 'Cuz I do. What do you really want from me? Why do you always have to put me down? Huh, Mamma?"

"I'm just telling you the truth, Parade. That hair and that makeup is not gonna change the person you are. I'm just being honest so when you go out there, you won't get your feelings hurt."

"Why get my feelings hurt out there when you crush them in here?"

I feel better as she leaves out my room. I close my door the moment her feet clear my doorway. I didn't mean to let her upset me, but it's hard not to sometimes. I wanted her to tell me that she liked my hair, that I'm pretty for once. Instead she tells me that she hates me even more.

I go from feeling beautiful to feeling like I'm walking around with shit smeared on my face. I decide it's time for me to get a job. One of the girls at the shop, Kristal, did say I can shampoo hair for her and she'll pay me under the table. I'm going to take her up on her offer because I can't absorb the hatred from my mother no more. I gotta get out of here.

Black and Ugly

"I did not, Sky. Why in the fuck would I call the cops on you? I wouldn't hurt you like that."

Is this the best day in my life gone wrong or what? First my mother and now this.

"Well who else told the cops we went to the party? I know you're probably mad because of what happened Sunday, but this is some bullshit, Parade."

"Are you even listening to me? I wouldn't do that to you, just 'cuz we got into a fight. What did they say anyway?"

"Basically, that they're investigating a few people about what happened that night. And, that next they'll be talking to Miss Daffany."

"Miss Daffany?"

"Yeah...so?"

"Sky, you know I'da never told them her name was Miss Daffany. They had to talk to Miss Wayne first. I'm sure they're questioning all of us and, I doubt he said anything either. Plus, he don't know nothing."

She's quiet, and I know she feels dumb for overlooking something so major. Only Miss Wayne calls people Miss before their name. The cops probably thought he was giving them our last names.

"Well…I'ma call him then," she says and hangs up.

She makes me so mad, sometimes. No "I'm sorry, Parade" or nothing and, all of this over me not letting her use my phone. I couldn't. If I had let her use my cell, she would have seen the words "Secret Lover" the moment she hit the send button Pretty soon I'm gonna have to leave Jay alone. But right now, I don't know how.

Speaking to Melvin earlier drained me. I don't want to be with him, but I'm afraid to let him go. Before I even started asking Jay for money, Melvin was paying for my cell phone and everything. But when he touches me, he makes my fucking skin crawl. I got to dump his ass.

"Parade, go walk to the store for your father. He needs some cough medicine."

"Ma, it's raining outside, and I don't want to mess my hair up."

"I don't give a fuck if you got your hair done or not. All you gonna do is fuck it up anyway."

"Can it wait till it dies down, please?"

"No…go now."

Black and Ugly

I instantly start crying. She knows I love my hair, and she wants me to mess it up on purpose. She doesn't want me to be happy for nothing. But why? I would do anything for my mother. I don't understand why she is so dead set on bringing me down all the damn time. I just take the money, run out the door and pray my umbrella will protect my hair.

"Excuse me, can I talk to you for a minute?" this guy asks from the driver seat of a red BMW with cream interior.

"Not really…I'm on my way to the store a few blocks up," I respond, not wanting to get closer to his car, only for him to realize I ain't attractive after all.

"Come on, beautiful. Let me take you to the store please."

Beautiful? Although that is the second time in a week someone has called me beautiful, I still figure he can't be talking to me

I move closer to his car with the umbrella in my left hand and bend down. I want him to see me. I want him to make sure that he still wants me to get into his car after he sees a close up of my face.

"What do you want with me?" I ask, talking through the rolled-down passenger window.

"For starters I want you to get your fine ass out the rain." He smiles.

I look him over real good before just jumping in his car. I haven't talked to a man that handsome since Jay. If he says the word, I'll be all over him.

I can't tell how tall he is but the way his knees are bent; I'll say he has to be over 6 feet tall. He's wearing a pair of sweatpants and two T-shirts. I love the way his chain falls against his chest and how he's rocking his shaped-up goatee and mustache. And, the smell of his car is an aphrodisiac. I've smelled this scent on Jay when he came to see me sometimes. I think its Black Ice tree freshener.

"Can I take you to where you're going, please? I hate to see beautiful women walk in the rain."

Whatever, I think.

"Okay...but don't try nothing," I say like I care if he does or not.

We're driving, and I notice his hairy arms. Although I am attracted to Jay's body, which is as smooth as a newborn baby, a man with hair always turns me on.

"So you live 'round here," he asks, "or do you just like walking in the rain in strange neighborhoods?"

"Unfortunately, I live around here. But, I ain't never seen this car or your face so I guess you don't."

"Naw...I'm here on some out-of-town business, and I'm renting this car because I got one just like it where I'm from, so it makes me feel at home."

"Oh." I smile, hoping Miss Wayne's honest about me having a pretty one. "What kind of business? Since you're renting a BMW, I take it...it must be serious," I add, wishing I had not made that comment.

Sky always says it's bama-fied when girls jock niggas just because of their rides. She thinks it's bad taste to compliment anybody on anything.

"I'm in the disposal business."

"What kind of disposal business?" I ask as my curiosity gets the best of me.

"The disposal of trash and junk that other folks don't feel like dealing with."

"Oh?" I hope I don't sound too stupid.

"What's your name, beautiful?"

"Please don't do that. Don't keep saying things that aren't true."

"First off, I don't say shit that ain't true. Now if you don't believe me, that's your hang up. But you are very attractive."

"And what's beautiful about me?" I ask, already sensing a lie coming on.

I mean I have a new hairstyle and everything, but it doesn't take away from my complexion or my face. I'm still the same ugly girl I was yesterday, only with hair.

"For one I love your smile. It's beautiful, you got all your teeth and everything," he jokes. "Secondly, I'm a man who loves chocolate women, so you're perfect. And that body...Damn!"

"You must be one of the only few men in the world who like dark-skin women," I say as he pulls up at the store.

"That's not true." He smiles. "There are plenty of dudes who appreciate chocolate, and there are a lot of brothers that don't. To be honest a beautiful woman is a beautiful woman."

"Is that right?" I smile.

"Yes, it is."

I'm so interested in him finding me attractive that I don't want to get out of the car. I play with the thought of him being here when I come back. Would he leave? Was this all a game? Did somebody pay him to mess with ugly Parade?

"You never did give me your name lil' lady."

"Parade," I reply, realizing he asked me that more than five minutes ago.

"Well, Parade, I think you are very beautiful and I don't have a reason to lie," he says and gives me a serious look. "I'd like to pick you up, take you out and

Black and Ugly

get to know you more. I *need* to get to know you more. You have any plans?"

"No," I respond, shocked that he still wants to hang out, even after having a close-up view of me. Maybe, the Maybelline makeup I bought works after all. I can't afford MAC just yet, even though Sky says it's the only makeup that really works.

"Well run into the store and get what you need." He hands me a $50 bill. "When you come back, we'll discuss our plans for this evening."

"Okay." I smile at the mystery man who wants to have something to do with me. "Did somebody pay you to meet me? Is this a joke?"

He looks at me and says, "This ain't no joke, Parade. I am very much interested in getting to know you more."

When I get out the car, I close the door gently and switch my curvaceous body as much as possible without going overboard. My body's the one thing I *know* is intact. And if he still wants to be bothered, after seeing me close up, I feel everything else will be a breeze.

CHAPTER 16

ECLIPSE (CANNON)

"I'm already here and already at work."

"Good. I left the money in your room, as well as pictures of the people you need to see."

"Yeah, I got it earlier. And just so you know, I work under the name Cannon."

"Cool with me. So what are your plans?" Smokes asks.

"Well, I work real slow, but I'm accurate," Eclipse says as he watches Parade's sexy body move within the store. "I like to visit only the people on my list and nobody else. I hope Silver told you that about me."

"Yeah, he did, and that's exactly what I need - something nice and quiet. They're already waiting on me to make a move."

"I'm glad you appreciate how I work," Eclipse says then pauses, "because I find that if you put people in certain positions, they'll tell you everything you need to know."

"Cool...look, your room at the Embassy Suites is paid up for a week. I take it that'll be enough."

"No, Mr. Parker," Eclipse states seriously, "that will not be enough. Now, I'll move as quickly as possible, but I don't get started until the second or third week."

"Well, how much you intend on charging me, man?" Smokes asks, sensing he's a rip-off. "Silver said you're expensive but damn."

"Mr. Parker, I'm a professional," he articulates real slowly. "You're paying for the job to be done right. Now in order for me to do that, I must go undetected. That's why I've been in business so long. I still have victim's relatives calling me now. You know why?" he asks then pauses. "Because they consider me family. Now if I go in a situation asking a bunch of questions, I'll draw attention to myself, unnecessary attention, and I can't have that. I befriend them, find out what I need to know then do what I do best. I'll leave knowing everything about them while, they'll know nothing about me."

Smokes is quiet but he appreciates how he's serious concerning handling business. He still thinks he's too expensive but at this time there is nothing he can do. Eclipse has already started working.

"And my prices are standard," he continues. "Fifteen thousand, and $50, not including my expenses."

"And $50? What's the $50 for?"

"For something else that just came up. I can tell you, with me coming out from Texas, I usually charge more than that. But since you know Silver, even though I don't trust him too much, I agreed to give you a discount on my prices. And after seeing how sexy one of my suspects is, it would be a shame to charge you full price."

"You must be talking about Sky," Smokes says.

"Naw...I'm talking about Parade."

"Parade? Yeah, okay. Maybe that's how you like them in Texas, but we like our women a little classier out here." He laughs, questioning his taste. "Just don't let that shit fuck with what I hired you to do."

"Does a man who goes to a business meeting over dinner with his associates avoid eating?"

"What?"

"I said does a man who takes his business associates out to eat avoid eating?"

"I don't know, nigga. But what's your fucking point?"

"My point is that although I'm gonna have fun with Parade, in the end if she's the one, she's done the moment I get off her."

"That's all I need to know."

"Enough said."

"Hey," Parade says as she gets in the car. "I didn't catch your name."

"My friends call me Cannon."

"Cannon?" She pauses. "I like that."

144 *Black and Ugly*

CHAPTER 17

SKY

If anything can be said about Jay its that he knows how to please me. He's passionate in the bedroom, and his money always flows. I can accept him ignoring me the way that he has lately, just as long as when we come together, he makes it worth my while.

My parents are out of town on business as usual. This is tight because it means we'll have the entire house to ourselves. I cut off all the lights and allow the ambience to flow from the candles. I also light some of that sweet smelling oil from Bath and Body Works throughout the house. And to top it all off, I have on my red La Perla undie set with my sexy red stilettos.

He opens the door and walks right in. I keep it open because he hates knocking on doors or standing in hallways, saying something about it gives niggas too much time to rush him. He's wearing a pair of jeans, a plain T-shirt and a jacket. His platinum chain, and soft hair, is the first thing I notice. I tell Jay all the time that he could be a model if he wanted to. He's that perfect - something like Ginuwine but a little bit taller. I can't help but think about how pretty our babies will be when we have some.

"Why you got all the lights out?" he asks as he closes the door, locks it and flips the light switch on.

"Because I'm trying to make love to my man, that's why," I say as I kiss him and turn the lights back off.

"Well, I ain't here for all that. I'm tired, plus, I can't stay too long."

"What you saying, Jay?" I ask, hoping he won't ruin our night before it even starts. "Is everything okay?"

"If you call my niece getting robbed cool then, yeah, okay. But the way I feel right now, I can smash somebody's skull in."

"Your niece Shannon? Is she okay?"

"Not really. Whoever the mothafucka was waiting on her in the hallway, robbed her and made her suck his dick. I'm telling you right now, I better not find out who that nigga is," he says as he walks in, puts his gun on the table and sits on the couch.

I know it's wrong to be mad, but I feel like his niece ruined our night. He does too much for her as far as I'm concerned, and whoever robbed her probably knew that. I know it's selfish, but Jay is *my* man. She got her own man. Let him worry about her problems.

He must see the disappointment in my face because he tells me to come and sit on his lap. I flop on him, and he squeezes me tight. There's something about when a man holds you that makes you feel like you're the safest in the whole wide world. Rubbing his hand up and down my thigh makes my pussy wet. If I can just keep his mind on me, maybe he'll forget all about what happened to his niece.

"I got something for you before I leave," he says as he kisses me softly on my lips.

"What is it?" I ask, excited by the thought alone. What I really wanted, I know he ain't gonna give me, and that's an engagement ring.

"It's what you always wanted, baby," he continues real smoothly.

"And that is?" I inquire, trying hard to push the idea out of my mind that he may actually gonna propose to me.

He reaches in his pocket and pulls out a wad of money, and places five $1,000 bills on the table. The first time I'd ever seen what a $1,000 bill looked like was a couple of weeks after I met Jay, the first time he broke me off. Any other time, I'd be smiling from ear to ear, but now the money don't excite me. I am starting to believe that all he is doing is paying me off, like I'm his prostitute or something.

Before I can say anything, I smell the same scent that was on his shirt before. Mad or not, I'm gonna say something to him. Because even if it isn't Parade he is dealing with, it's definitely another woman.

"Jay! Why you smell like perfume?"

His eyes widen, and he begins to smell different parts of his shirt. I know what he's trying to do, buy time, but it ain't gonna work. I'm five seconds from banging him in his face.

"Uh...I don't smell nothing girl," he answers as he moves me off him. "Every time I come over here, it's some bullshit."

Pushing me off doesn't do anything but make me angrier. I jump on top of him and grab his shirt. I planned to be on top of him tonight anyway, but not like this. I know I look like a madwoman trying to fight him in my underwear, but I don't care.

"Jay! You tell me right now what the fuck is up. I'm tired of your shit. I smelled this same smell the last time we went to the movies. I think you stepping out on me, so be a man and tell me what's really up."

"Bitch, you tripping. I'm getting tired of your shit anyway. All you gonna do is make me cut your ass off," he yells as he stands.

"Cut me off? Cut me off? Who the fuck you think you talking to, Jay? You wish you could cut a bitch like me off."

"Are you serious?" he asks and starts laughing. "You ain't nothing but a high-class hoe," he says then moves toward the door.

"Fuck you, Jay. There's plenty of niggas who would want to be with me. I'm telling you right now, if you leave out the door, it's over between us. And you won't never taste this sweet pussy again," I yell as I block him before he reaches the door.

He walks back toward the couch and I think my threat works, as usual. I know Jay doesn't want to be with nobody but me. He's handsome and all, but I'm far from a slouch too. So although he's trying to play it off, losing me will hurt a lot. I'm sure of it.

"I guess you won't be needing this then, will you?" he asks as he grabs the money off the table. "Tell them punk-ass niggas you fuck with to take care of you, bitch. It's over," he continues as he walks out and slams the door.

CHAPTER 18

DAFFANY

Waking up this morning feels weird. I rise and the hairs on my back stand up the moment I throw the covers off me. Although my door is closed, I have the strange feeling that someone is in my room or the apartment. I fall back down on the bed and dive under the covers. I don't move. I can't if I want to. I wait for the light to sneak under my blinds to give me proof that I'm alone.

An hour later, but still early in the morning, the sun eases me a little. But what is this feeling? Maybe, it's the E-pills I be on all the time. I gotta stop that shit sooner or later because it has gotten me in more trouble than I can count.

I move toward my bedroom door and open it. Now the feeling is so strong that if somebody is standing right in front of me, I won't be surprised. I walk to the kitchen with my back toward my living room. It feels scary, like the feeling I only get when I watch horror movies alone. It overtakes me.

I rinse off a cup and don't lift my head so that my eyes can wander into the dark living room. I'ma start leaving these fucking blinds open more often.

Eventually I focus on two things. First, I see the dark figure sitting in my living room on the chair in the corner. My heart is beating so fast, that it's preventing me from doing what I need to do, get the fuck out and save my own life. Next, I see the door move slightly open every time somebody leaves the building door or out of their apartment. My lock is popped. That's how he got in. But why is he still here?

My worst fear is realized as he says, "Get the fuck over here before I blow your fucking head off."

He demands my attention, so I have to look at him. I have to face him. Why the fuck he ain't just take what he wants and leave? Maybe, he realized that outside of that 32-inch TV, I really ain't got shit. Maybe, he's pissed because I sleep with my door locked and he couldn't get in while the only little money I have stays on me. But, that don't make any sense 'cuz he could have broken the bedroom door just like he came into the apartment.

"Now walk over here and sit the fuck down." He is serious, so serious, that if I don't comply and try to run for the door, he'll kill me instantly. I know it.

I walk toward the farthest chair from him, the one closest to the door in case I build up enough courage to go for it anyway.

"I been sitting in this house all night, since you went to sleep. How the fuck can you sleep? How can you lay your head down knowing what the fuck you did to me?"

I know him. Oh my God, I know him but why me? Why is he here? It's Cliff Shaun, my next-door neighbor. I turn tricks with him sometimes when his wife isn't home. Cliff is always nice because, sometimes, he just wants to talk. And, he'll pay me $150 to listen and maybe give him some head afterwards, but even that's always quick.

He's clean, nice and always considerate. He never makes me feel like a whore and I consider him one of my main customers so losing his business is so important to me. It could possibly mean having a phone or the lights turned off.

"I don't know what you're talking about, Cliff. What's going on? You're scaring me."

"I'M SCARING YOU? I'M FUCKING SCARING YOU? WHAT ABOUT ME?" He says as he jumps up and sits on the couch right next to me. His eyes are red and swollen, and he looks like he's been crying all night.

I'm trembling. Shaking so badly that I feel myself getting ready to pee right where I sit. I know if he yells at me again, it will be all over my floor and the cloth chair I'm sitting in.

"Cliff, please tell me what's wrong. Maybe, I can help you. Maybe I can help you get out of whatever trouble you're in. Did your wife find out about us? I can tell her it's not true. I don't have no problem with it, Cliff."

I'm pleading my case, but he looks like a demon just ready to rip my soul from my body and tear it into pieces.

"Get dressed, Daffany. Put your fucking clothes on and get dressed," he tells me.

I always knew that you are never supposed to leave with someone when they have a gun. You're supposed to stay right where you are and scream your ass off because if you leave, it's all over anyway. 'Cuz, for real, you will die.

I wonder if the same thing goes for this scenario since we're in my apartment. Technically, nobody's here, and he can easily do whatever he wants and no one would know. My friends won't even come by until 12 or 1 o'clock.

"Where are we going, Cliff?" I ask, slowly and carefully as to not piss him off any worse.

"We're going to the free clinic. I wanna know if you got it or not. I wanna know if you got the same shit you gave to my wife, our unborn child and me. I wanna know if you are that vicious to do some bullshit like that to me. That's where we're going. I wanna know if you're the reason my fucking life will never be the same. So get fucking dressed!"

I'm feeling weak. I can't keep my head up. I'm dizzy...I...

I come to and my robe is off but I have on some mismatched pants and shirt. I'm even wearing a pair of tennis I never wore. I focus as my eyes meet the sun coming through the open blinds. Did I lunch out off the 'E' I took last night. Am I still having reactions?

I turn around to look at the door and the same fear that overtook me before I blacked out is back again. Then I realize he has gotten me dressed. He's dead set on taking me out of this apartment. What's scarier is that, although he's probably still here, I feel safer inside than I do out there. My lock is still broken, only now it's taped shut, I guess to prevent it from moving every time somebody comes in or out of their apartment.

Black and Ugly

"You up, bitch?" he asks as he walks out of the bathroom. "I took the liberty of going through your shit. I don't see nothing pertaining to HIV in your apartment. Tell me you got it and we ain't gotta go to no fucking clinic. Tell me you got the shit and stop wasting my mothafucking time. Tell me the truth, Daffany."

"I don't know what's going on. I mean, I'm sorry about your wife and baby and all, but I ain't got no HIV, Cliff."

"Well who in the fuck gave it to me then?" he yells as spit escapes his mouth to meet mine. "I thought this was cool. I thought this was real cool, keeping time the way we did. I felt like you helped save my marriage. For real, before you, I ain't wanna touch my wife. Maybe, I ain't know how to touch her no more. We fought too fucking much to wanna do anything with each other, let alone touch," he says as he drinks a glass of orange juice, he got out my fridge.

"I found out I had the shit from a routine checkup," he explains as he stops and looks at me again. "A routine checkup." He laughs. "Ain't that something? Now my fucking routine checkups will pertain to checking my T cell count and shit. I figured, after finding out I had it, that maybe it was my punishment for being unfaithful to my wife. But then..." he continues and starts to cry hysterically.

"But then...She got a prenatal checkup and found out she's infected. It's fucking *positive* that she has HIV. I gave her that shit because I fucked with you," he insists.

"But Cliff...you even said yourself you were seeing somebody else. Uh...remember?" I say, not knowing if it's a good idea to mention at this point.

"But, you're a fucking whore. Everybody know that fucking whores carry that shit," he yells. "I didn't get it from nobody else."

His words hurt, although they should have bounced off me like a bad check. I am what I am. But I didn't want to have it confirmed by a man who was always kind up until this point. That rips my heart apart.

"I don't want to hear that shit," he continues. "As a matter fact..." he says then pauses and pulls the gun out his pocket. "I don't feel like talking no more. Get the fuck up and let's leave. The clinic downtown will tell you, right then and there, if you're positive or not. And if you are, I'ma kill you, the doctor and anybody else in that mothafucka."

Why is this happening to me? I can't go with him. I just cannot do it. He's made it clear that the moment I step out that door HIV positive that I ain't coming back. Also, more people could end up dead.

"Look, I'm not leaving out that door. You're not sane, and you're not acting right. You done broke in my fucking apartment, went through my shit and now you're telling me I got something I don't know nothing about. And, you want me to get in the car with you? Now, I'm sorry about Lashonda having that shit and I'm really sorry about you having it, too, but it ain't me. And I'm not leaving my apartment."

I don't know where that came from. And, I certainly don't feel as bold as I sound, but he's holding me at gunpoint and threatening to shoot other mothafuckas. I can't be down with that shit.

Without saying another word, he grabs me by my neck and steals me. He punches me in my stomach, and my face again, two times in the eye. I count twelve blows. I almost don't feel anything anymore. Just drifting, something like floating but not quite. Maybe, it's for the best that he kills me. Because if he don't, I'ma still do what I gotta do to make a living. I mean...somebody gave me this shit too. And for all I know, it could've been him. He hit me one last time.

CHAPTER 19

PARADE

I am running late, cuz my mother makes me go to the store again. "Pick me up some peas, Parade," she says when I accidentally answer my cell phone, thinking it's Cannon.

She's so jealous she don't know what to do. I've been keeping time with Cannon ever since I met him a few days ago. I cut Melvin off for good after asking him to give me some money. I spent most of mine on my hair and the rest went to my mother. He had the nerve to tell me no so I decided it was no use being bothered with his short, stubby ass, cuz outside of giving me a few dollars, he doesn't do much for me.

Tonight, Cannon wants to take me out and meet my mother. I'm nervous but, in a way, I want her to see him. I decide against it because I'm afraid she'll embarrass me. But, she would fall out when she sees how handsome he is. Model material, baby.

We even had a couple walk over to our table, at Jaspers restaurant one night, to tell us we look good together. That has never happened to me in my life but I would've been pissed if somebody told me that *Melvin* and I made a nice couple. Yuck! I haven't even seen my friends like I use to 'cuz we've been together everyday. And anyway, I've seen enough of them bitches to last me a lifetime. Yesterday, Cannon pressed me though, saying he wants to get to know everybody that's important to me. No man has ever cared about getting to know my friends and family in the past, but he does.

I make it back to the building and I'm almost at the apartment door when Markee busts in.

"Excuse me. Can I talk to you for a minute?"

Uuuuggghhh! What did he want? He knows I can't stand to look at him, let alone talk to him.

I reluctantly turn around and say, "What, Markee? I'm meeting someone later."

"Parade, is that you? Awwwww shit. I'm all ready to lay down game and that's your fine ass. Damn, girl, you looking good as shit. *Dayumm!*"

"Thank you, Markee...I think," I respond, wanting to unlock my door, but not wanting him to be on crud time and bust up in there with me.

"Girl...you gotta let me take you out," he shouts.

In a way, I'm happy he's making so much noise because if something happens to me, maybe someone will hear. That's one thing that's messed up about the Manor. If you have a conversation in the hallway, everyone can hear it because of the echo.

"Markee, you like five years old," I tell him, unenthused by his compliments.

"Who the fuck you talking to, joe? Don't ever fucking call me a kid again. I'm more man than any of them niggas you fuck wit,' for real," he says as the transformation of the killer I know exists emerges through in his voice.

"Nobody, Markee. It's not that serious," I tell him.

"Take my number, and call me when you get a chance," he continues, softening his face a little.

I'm scared of him and he knows everybody around this mothafucka is scared of him, especially girls. Plus, he just smacked a girl 'cuz she wouldn't give him her number. I consider myself lucky because he didn't ask for mine. See, I don't have no problems fighting a dude but you can't win if they have a gun.

"Okay." I wait for him to give me his number so he can leave.

"I ain't got no pen, young. Get one out your purse," he tells me.

The look on my face says what's on my mind. I don't feel comfortable reaching in my purse for anything while he's here. I ain't taking the chance of my money Jay gave me yesterday dropping out and him robbing me in my hallway.

"I ain't gonna fuck with you, young," he reassures me.

Black and Ugly

I reach in my purse and carefully pull out a pen, making sure not to rattle the loose bills.

"Wayne fucking with purses again?" he asks.

"What?"

"Is Wayne fucking with purses again?" he repeats, looking at the new Louis Vuitton that I am sporting.

Yes, he is but no, I ain't gonna tell him. There is no way on earth I'll tell this fool that Miss Wayne is doing something. He's my closest friend and the only one out the group who truly cares about how I feel. He gave me two purses the other day, just 'cuz he likes me to have nice things.

"What?" he says with a devious look on his face. "You think I robbed Wayne?" he continues telling on himself. "Don't believe that shit, man. That's just a rumor. Whoever broke in his house tried to set me up, and shit, by leaving my high school ID. What I look like dropping that shit? That's just asking to get caught."

I'm not convinced, so I ain't buying it. I just hand him the pen and a napkin I had in my purse. He writes down his number, which will soon find my trash.

"No," I state, remembering to tie up loose ends before he tries to rob Miss Wayne again. "Wayne's not fucking with that shit no more. My new friend gave me this."

"You not talking about that nigga whose car been out front lately, are you?" he asks as he smiles like the joke is on me.

"Yeah, why?" I inquire, irritated with his short ass.

"Don't fall for that nigga, Parade. He's here on business," he continues as he hands me the napkin.

"Yeah, I know. He told me," I respond.

"He ain't tell you shit. Trust me. I know what I'm talking 'bout." He smirks.

"Okay, Markee." I wave my hand.

"Put the number in your cell phone. You might lose that napkin," he commands. "I'll wait."

I hurry up and put the right number in the phone and store it in case he wants to see it. At this point, he can do whatever he desires 'cuz I'm tired of his shit. I don't want to hear anything he has to say about Cannon fucking with some girl around the neighborhood because that's not gonna stop me from messing with him.

"You think I'm playing? You'll see. When that nigga finish doing what need to be done, you call me. I know more shit than you think I do. I know everything around here."

"Alright, Markee." I approach my door. "I gotta go."

"Get at me later," he responds leaving the building.

I walk in the house and throw my purse on the kitchen counter. Markee makes me sick with his young ass. I'm trying to talk to Cannon, not waste time with him in the funky ass hallway. I'm about to call Cannon's fine ass but I notice a note, on a sticky piece of paper, by the phone.

Parade,
Daffany is in P.G. County Hospital. She was hurt really badly.
Wayne and Sky said they'll meet you there.
Dad

What happened to my friend? I pick up the phone and call a cab. I'm so nervous. Is she okay? Did one of them niggas she fuck with hurt her? I wanted Daffany out of that life anyway. And when did Miss Wayne call? I just hope I'm not too late. The cab arrives; I grab my purse and run out the door.

CHAPTER 20

SKY

Seeing how bad Daffany is fucks me up. We have our problems, but I never want to see her like this. And if I hadn't left my jacket, the night they pissed me off, I would have never known she was there...half dead. The door, being slightly opened, scared me and I knew, immediately, that something was up.

I've walked up on a half-open door before when I was younger. And I will never forget what I saw.

I was 10 years old and was on my way to my favorite uncle's house. Unlike the rest of my mother's side of the family, Uncle Rickie always told me how pretty I was. Everybody else on my mother's side hated on me. They hated on both of us. They'd say shit like "just 'cuz you light, don't mean you pretty."

See, everybody on my mother's side is brown skin and thinks that if you're light skin you think you're

Black and Ugly

cute. It ain't my fault most lighter people are. It's just the way it is. It hurts me a lot because my cousins get all the love from family because of their brown complexion.

But, Uncle Rickie showed me the attention he knew I wasn't getting from them. He'd kiss me on my lips and tell me I was the prettiest niece he had. It wasn't nothing for him to come home with a big-ass Toys R Us bag filled with stuff *only* for me. "Give Uncle Rickie a kiss," he'd tell me, and I'd give him the biggest kiss I could.

Uncle Rickie was always affectionate like that but my mother, who if you asked me was just jealous, said it wasn't appropriate for him to kiss and hug me that way. What way? I use to cry, because I never understood why she wouldn't let me show him how much I loved him. He never lifted my skirt or any of that other shit you hear about on TV. All he ever did was show me he cared about me. I would sit on his lap, and he'd read me stories while telling me how pretty I was in my ear.

But, I didn't know Uncle Rickie was into drugs. I just thought he was rich. It was with him that I was first introduced to fashion. He'd give me any designer label I asked for and, even the stuff I didn't. He kept me up on all the latest gear so every Saturday, like clockwork, I'd go to Uncle Rickie's. He lived in the same complex.

So, rushing to be with my favorite uncle on Saturday was very important to me, something that I always looked forward to. But, one day I walked up on his building, eager to tell him about the beauty contest I won in school, because I knew he'd be happy for me and give me a present. His door was slightly open.

I pushed it farther and could see clear through a large, gaping hole in my uncle's head. I was terrified and couldn't stay by myself for months. My mom would pay Miss Wayne or Daffany's mom to let me stay with them until they made it home from work. But, I never got over how it felt to see my uncle that way. I still have nightmares now.

Approaching Daffany's apartment gave me similar feelings. She was beaten so badly that I couldn't see her face because it was covered in her own blood. Daffany really needs to get protection if she's gonna stay in that game. She really needs to get someone to look after her when she's turning tricks. But, she wants to do everything herself. She wouldn't even be open to the

Black and Ugly

idea of having that type of scenario, if she was willing to work with someone. Maybe, when she comes around, she'll see that she needs me more than she thinks she does.

"Whoever laid her tracks did a damn good job," Jewel says as we look at the back of a girl who is talking to the hospital receptionist. Her hair moves every time she does. It's bouncy and it makes me wanna throw some long tracks up in mine.

Although I'm far from gay, I have to admit that she has a nice body, too, almost as sexy as mine. And I'm feeling that new Louis Vuitton purse she's sporting. It's the same one I want. I will definitely have to tell Miss Wayne to cop that for me.

He's kinda stingy sometimes, though. I always figured since he's stealing anyway, he'd give me a cheaper price or, maybe even throw in two purses for the price of one but not him. He'll say they're special order and he's already giving them to me as cheap as he can. I know he's into me hard because of Jay. Sometimes, he's more worried about what was in my man's pockets than I am.

"Ain't that the Manhattan GM by Louis she's rocking?" Jewel asks.

"Yeah, girl," I tell her. "I need that purse in my life."

She turns and walks in our direction and I'm furious when I see the girl we've been jocking for the past few minutes is Parade. Oh, I'm heated. Her hair looks good and she's wearing a fresh pair of Evisu jeans with the matching fitted tee, topped off with the oversized belt and a new pair of Fendi boots. BITCH! Miss Wayne's a bitch, too. I bet he ain't charging Parade for none of that shit. I know she couldn't have gotten it from nowhere else.

"Hey, girl," Parade says as she walks over and hugs me, wearing the same perfume that grosses me out now. "How she doing?"

I return a fake ass hug and reply, "I don't know. They won't let us in since we're not family."

"We are family," she yells, looking like she's getting ready to cry. "What the fuck they mean? They don't have no idea of how close we are," she questions as she takes the seat right next to me. "Hey, Jewel."

Silence.

I knew Jewel was gonna do that, on account of me telling her that I thought Parade is after Jay. But, I didn't tell her that I wasn't sure if he wanted her too. It's too embarrassing to think the thought let alone say the words. I mean... Jay wanting stinky 'lil Parade, who always jocked my style, is unbelievable to me.

"*Okay...*" Parade says, ignoring Jewel's rudeness. "Where's Miss Wayne?"

168   *Black and Ugly*

"He downstairs getting something to drink," I answer, still not trying to talk to her too much.

I'm still trying to figure out what she told Miss Wayne and Daffany about the night of the murder. Even though the cops only asked me a few questions, I'm not sure if I can trust her.

"Who did your hair?" I ask.

"Carol," she responds, excited that I noticed. "You like it?"

"It's okay...She should have tightened up the front a little more, but it's okay for you," I utter, trying to carry her.

She puts her head down and I can tell I got to her. I need to keep Parade in her place. I don't want her thinking she's better than me because, if she wants to be in my league, she will have a hell of a lot of work to do.

"Good one," Jewel whispers real low. "That bitch still not better than you."

"What the fuck you just say?" Parade lifts her head up and looks at Jewel.

Jewel doesn't move. Her eyes get two sizes too big because she didn't think Parade heard her. She's also scared to death of Parade, knowing all the stories I've told her about how Parade always has my back and is quick to stomp a bitch out.

"Nothing...uh...I ain't say nothing," Jewel states.

I don't want to say anything, but Jewel is embarrassing me a little. Now, Parade will know that I roll with a punk ass bitch.

"Oh, you said something, bitch," Parade says as she takes off her earrings and put them in the purse I'm hating her for. "Don't eat your words now. I ain't feed them to you yet."

I'm so happy to see Miss Wayne get off the elevators, with his pink Capri set and matching heels that I don't know what to do.

"Miss Parade," he yells, reaching out for her.

Parade takes her eyes off Jewel, for one second, to greet him and then coldly lay them back on her.

"You look beautiful, girl. My baby looks like a model, don't she, Sky?"

In my opinion, she looks *okay* but she can't win no contest.

"Thanks, Miss Wayne," Parade says while looking back at Jewel. "Let me tell you something bitch. I don't know what Sky's been telling you, but I take that shit from her, 'cuz I love her. She's like family. But don't you think, for one minute, that I wouldn't put my foot in your ass, quick. Believe that."

"Maybe, I ought to leave," Jewel responds.

"Maybe you better, chile," Miss Wayne adds.

"I'll call you later, Sky." Jewel rushes toward the elevator. I know she's happy it's open.

"Miss Sky, I leave you for five minutes and you 'bout to have Miss Parade fighting again. That chile is already funny looking. We don't want Miss Parade to make things worse, now do we?" He laughs. "Baby, you look fierce, and your face is beat," he says as he snaps his fingers looking Parade over again. "Miss Sky, what happened anyway?" He has one hand on Parade's back, trying to calm her down. "What you do to her?" He looks at me. "Fuck it. It don't even matter. I ain't seen you in days, Miss Parade. I miss you. I wanna see you, too you know."

He's giving her a lot. I haven't seen him in a while, either, and I ain't get none of that shit.

"Who been keeping you busy?" he asks as he gently touches her shoulder to sit her back down in the chair. "Tell me all about him. And don't leave nothing out. I wanna hear dick size and all, honey. I ain't had none, since yesterday, so believe me, I'm long overdue." He laughs.

"Well, I do have a new friend. He's so handsome, Miss Wayne. I really can't wait for ya'll to meet him. He drives a red BMW and, since Tuesday, we've spent everyday together," Parade explains.

I don't believe her. I mean…she looks better. I'll give her that, but she ain't pulling no balling ass nigga. And whoever he is, he'll be gone the moment she fucks him. Please believe.

"Did you give him the goods, chile? And don't hold back," Miss Wayne inquires as he moves his hands. I swear he can't say a word without 'em.

"Yes...and it is good. We've done it every night since I met him," Parade continues while looking at me for approval. "He looks like somebody who would want Sky, not me."

"Girl, please." I wave her off. "I'm sure he isn't my type."

"You're probably right." She smiles. "Let's not fight, Sky. I miss you. I miss not being able to talk to you and tell you about my life. Let's not keep this up no more."

Miss Wayne is looking at me like; *you better accept my baby's apology.* But, I'm not sure if I want to just yet. There are still a lot of unanswered questions. A whole lot. Before I can think about it anymore, the two officers who have hassled me, ever since that bitch died, shows up.

"Oh my goodness, what are you two doing here?" Miss Wayne asks.

"We're here because this beating seemed very suspicious. We figured you all could tell us if it's related to the murder the other night," Officer Oakley responds.

"Don't come here with that shit. We don't feel like it right now," Parade yells.

Black and Ugly

I know then that they've been bothering them just as much as they've harassed me. And by the sound of her voice, Parade ain't told them nothing.

"Yes, boys. We're here to support our friend, not be harassed with the likes of you. Now, if you would, please excuse us. You two are in our way," Miss Wayne finishes.

"We'll leave you alone for now. Have a nice day," Officer Oakley says.

"You too," Miss Wayne yells as she scans them with his eyes.

"Okay...which one of them you fucked?" Parade asks after they got on the elevator.

"Why would you say that?" he questions as he covers his mouth with his fingers appearing shocked.

"Because I could see something in your eyes," Parade responds.

"Officer D. Hurts, baby." Miss Wayne laughs and he puts his hand on his chest. "And boy did it hurt. He was coming by tonight but after my baby got beat up, there was just a change of plans," he continues as the laughter in his voice slowly diminishes.

"You think she looked bad now," I say. "You should have seen her when I found her."

After sitting in the waiting area for what seemed like days, the doctor tells us that Daffany is fine and, outside of the physical bruises, she suffered a minor contusion. He's keeping her overnight for further observation, but says she is conscious and asking for us. We walk in her room and don't say a word. The four of us just hold one another and cry.

CHAPTER 21

DAFFANY

Coming home feels eerie and uncomfortable, but I have to face my fears. I needed to come home. I guess I can stay with Miss Wayne if I want to. Don't think he didn't ask me five or six times either. I considered it, too, because I'm terrified that Cliff will come back to hurt me some more or even finish me off. Imagine living next door to the man who assaulted you, knowing your apartment will never be safe again. What will happen when the disease gets worse? Will he come back and beat me each time something goes wrong? It's a fucked up way to feel about the place you call home.

"Be careful, girl," Parade says as she helps me up the stairs. "Hold on to the rail."

I'm so happy to see how pretty Parade looks. The long tracks soften her features and the makeup she's wearing makes her complexion appear even.

"Thanks, Parade. You don't know how much I appreciate you doing this for me."

"You would've done the same thing for me. You're my sister," she says.

She hands me the keys to the new lock that the rental office replaced after I told them what happened from the hospital. I open the door and remain in the hallway. Parade, sensing I'm scared, goes in before me to check things out. She's smiling but her smile is slowly diminishing as she walks in and out of each room.

"What?" I ask her, feeling scared. "What's going on?"

"Daffany...uh...everything is fine. But...uh...all your things are gone," she stutters.

"What?" I ask as I walk in after confirming it's safe. "What do you mean my things are gone?" I continue then close the door and lock it behind me.

I walk into my apartment and I see it's almost empty. My couch, my TV, some of my kitchen supplies and a few other things that use to be in my living room are all gone.

I quickly run to my bedroom to see if anything is missing from in there. Parade walks behind me, waiting to console me in case I break down. I enter the room to see my mattress pushed to the side, exposing part of the box spring underneath it. I push the mattress completely away looking for the papers I had confirming my HIV status. I kept some money there, too but I knew that was gone the moment I saw the bed.

The papers are gone. There's nothing left except air. I just fall to the mattress, on the floor and start crying.

"Daffany," Parade calls as she rushes to my side, "it'll be okay. We can replace all this stuff." She holds me and rocks me. "Don't worry about it. We can make your place just like new."

I lie in Parade's arms, pretending like the tears really are about my stolen things. Truth is, they can have all that shit. But, the papers confirming the vicious disease mutating inside my body are my property. It was the one secret I didn't want to share with anyone but now someone out there, besides me, knows.

"Parade," I whisper between my wiping tears, "can you help me get to Miss Wayne's house? I can... I can't stay here tonight."

"Sure," She helps me up and we move toward the door.

CHAPTER 22

SKY

"Where you at, bitch?" Jewel yells at me through the phone.

I allow her to call me a bitch, although I hate it. Parade and them don't even talk to me like that and I've known them all my life. Well, Miss Wayne does sometimes, but that's just how he is.

"At PG Plaza. I'm picking up a few things for H20 tonight. We still going right?"

"Yeah, it's on."

"Why you ask anyway?"

"'Cuz I'm sitting at your complex and I see this fine-ass nigga with your fake-ass friend Parade. She just went in the house, and he's leaning up against a BMW, girl. Damn, he looks edible."

"For real?" I respond all excited at the possibility of a snatch coming along. "What he look like? I swear I thought Parade was lying about her new man."

"She definitely ain't lying if she said he's handsome. Well he's about Jay's height. And, right now, he's wearing his cap pulled all the way down. All you can see is his sexy ass lips. Sky, I want him for myself, girl."

Black and Ugly

Jewel says that and suddenly I have an idea. I want to see if Parade's boyfriend will take the bait if Jewel tries to hit on him. If I were there, I'd do it myself. I'm pretty sure he'll like Jewel because, unlike Parade, Jewel has her own salon, her own car and a lot of other good shit going for herself. Not to mention, Jewel is much easier on the eyes.

"You should do it, Jewel," I instigate, trying to convince her to walk over to him.

"Do what?"

"Try to talk to him."

"But…uh…what if that girl comes back out while I'm still talking to him? I ain't trying to whip her ass tonight, Sky."

Whip her ass? Yeah, right. That's her way of telling me she's scared to death. I can't stand a scary bitch. Parade has her so shook that she's afraid to say anything to her man.

"If you hurry up, she won't see you. It ain't like you know who her man is anyway. For all you know, he's some dude hanging outside. So if she comes out, just step off."

"I ain't doing all that, Sky. I mean he looks fuckable but I'm not pressed either."

"Please," I beg.

She's quiet for a minute and I can tell she's definitely considering it. Truthfully, I'm not use to begging somebody to do something I want them to do. That's another thing I miss about Parade. If I give the word she's on it like a pit bull no matter what.

"Okay. I'll call you back."

"Uhn-ahn, bitch. I'm staying on the phone. I want to hear everything."

"Okay. I'll hold the phone in my hand."

"Good."

I can hear her footsteps as she walks over to him. I'm mad that she got off the phone so quick because I was gonna give her some pointers on what to say. But, I figure she's a fly bitch whose use to dealing with fly niggas so that might not even be necessary.

A few seconds go by and I hear, "Excuse me. You live around here?"

He don't say nothing more than, "Naw."

"Oh. Well...uh...I should've known that. I would've remembered seeing somebody who looks like you."

Somebody who looks like you? What the fuck is Jewel talking about?

"And why is that?" he questions in a voice so sexy it makes my pussy jump.

"Because somebody that looks like you would've been with somebody that looks like me, that's why."

That's a weak ass line, deserving exactly what it gets, silence.

Black and Ugly

"Listen, sweetheart. I got my eye on somebody else right now."

"Somebody who looks better than me?" Jewel asks.

Get 'em, girl. 'Cuz you know that bitch ain't got nothing on you.

"Somebody who's just as fine as you are," he replies.

"Oh," she says as if she's disappointed.

"Look, I can't lie, I'm feeling her. So, unfortunately, I can't go any further with you other than saying you're a beautiful woman who at any other time would've been on my arm."

"Oh. I see."

"I'm sorry," he continues.

"Naw, it's cool. I understand. I hope ya'll are happy."

"We are. Trust me." I feel his smile coming through Jewel's phone.

She gets back to her car sounding irritated and mad that I put her up to approach him, only to get knocked down. Just like me she isn't use to being rejected. She looked just like Amerie with her real hair falling within the small of her back.

"Girl, I just got carried," she says real low. "I can't believe you made me do that shit."

"I know. I heard it."

"How the fuck he gonna choose Parade instead of me?" Jewel yells. "He must be gay."

"Well if he's dealing with Parade, he's definitely not gay."

"Whatever that bitch doing it's working."

"Well, he ain't met me yet."

"And what does that suppose to mean? You saying you look better than me or something?"

"You know I do, girl. And anyway, I'm on my way to the house so I'll see you in a minute." I hang up the phone.

Is it possible that Parade really has come up after all? Naw.

CHAPTER 23

PARADE

I've never had a man make love to me like Cannon does. *Ever.* It seems like we've had sex every day since the first day I met him. Kissing my neck gently he backs me up against the wall until I'm forced to inhale his cologne.

"What are you wearing, baby?" I whisper.

"You. I'm wearing you. You like it?" He kisses me softly on the lips.

Damn, this man says the right things. He begins to slowly unzip my pants as he runs his warm hand across my stomach. Judging by how big his dick is growing in his jeans I can tell he likes what he feels. He slides my pants all the way to the floor and, one by one, I remove my legs until I stand half-naked against the hotel room wall. Cannon backs up, flips the light switch on and observes my body.

"Do you know how beautiful you are?" he asks as if he wants to eat me up.

I don't answer. I can't risk saying anything that will ruin this moment. He places his hat on the table, walks up to me and I help him remove his shirt. As I run my fingers between the muscle grooves on his chest my pussy becomes wetter and wetter. His shirt is completely off so I unzip his jeans exposing his Versace boxer briefs.

His big black dick is waiting to enter my horny body and I'm waiting for it too. On my knees, I remove his pulsating dick from his briefs and wrap my lips around it. I suck every inch of him. His sweet pre-cum lines the surface of my throat.

"This feels so good, baby," he moans. "Damn."

Leading him to the bed, I remove my shirt and get on all fours. I want this night to be everything he wants it to be.

"It's like that," he says then gently spreads my ass cheeks to get a good glimpse of my pussy.

"Yeah. It's just like that," I moan seductively as I pump my hips.

He licks his middle finger and sticks it gently inside me and I fuck it as if it's his dick. I can tell, by the look on his face, that he's getting aroused even more. He glances at me the way Jay does when he's ready to cum inside me.

"Come on, baby. Fuck this ugly black pussy."

He stares at me and uses his body to push me toward the bed. I smile at first, thinking it's another freaky game, until I see the look in his eyes. I wonder what ruined the moment.

"What? What's wrong?"

184   *Black and Ugly*

"Baby, why you keep saying that every time we have sex?"

"Saying what?"

"That you're ugly."

I grab the sheets on the bed to cover my naked body. I'm embarrassed by his question. I only said what I thought he wanted to hear. When I'm with Jay, and the others, they preferred me to say that during sex.

"I don't know. 'Cuz it's true, I guess."

"Naw, it's not. And I need you to stop saying that," he demands as he reaches in and kisses my lips. "You insulting me. I wouldn't be with you if you weren't fine."

Cannon's words make me desire him even more. I pull him on top of me and place his dick gently in my pussy. My mouth opens because, for one minute, I forgot how good it feels to have him inside of me.

Swiftly but smoothly, he moves in and out of my wet, throbbing pussy. I've never heard a man call my name and make it sound so good before. I'm just about to cum when he places his warm mouth on my ear and whispers to me, "I wish things could be different."

Before I can ask him what he means, I feel a tingling sensation take over me as I explode all over his thick black dick. We hold each other closely and drift off to sleep.

By T. Styles   185

CHAPTER 24

PARADE

"What are you doing to me, boy?" I ask as I sweep Daffany's kitchen floor while holding my cell phone with my shoulder. "Don't spoil me then leave me by myself, all fucked up in the head, when you go back home."

"I'm not trying to spoil you, beautiful. I'm just giving you what you deserve. Is something wrong with that?" Cannon asks.

"No," I respond and I smile. "And you definitely treated me better, in the past few weeks, than most men have all my life. I'm gonna miss you when you leave. Damn! Has it only been a few weeks, for real? It feels like forever," I continue, feeling emotional at the thought of the man, belonging only to me, leaving in the next couple of days.

"Yes, it's only been a few weeks, baby."

I've learned little about Cannon over the past few weeks. One thing I did discover is that he doesn't take to me questioning him about his home life or the specifics of his business. Normally, that might make me a little suspicious but he's so nice to me that I don't care.

I mean we haven't known each other but a couple of weeks and already he's spent money on me as if it's nothing - doing stuff like taking me to dinner at expensive restaurants, telling me to order whatever I want on the menu and letting me pick out outfits at Macy's so I can look presentable when I start my new job at Carol's shop next week.

The things he does shows he cares about me more than anything else and I'm already starting to trust him with my heart. Don't get me wrong, I've gotten use to having my share of cash lately, because of Jay but Cannon does stuff for me because he cares not because he's trying to control me. I know Jay does it trying to keep me on his leash.

"I want to talk to you about something serious, baby," Cannon says with the tone of his voice matching his statement.

"Okay," I respond, hoping he won't end what we have just yet.

"I'm falling for you," he continues as his words cause me to walk to the living room to sit down. "And, I'm very serious."

I feel that if I move to another room I will come to my senses and realize I didn't hear what he said correctly. Maybe he said he didn't want me falling for him like Jay told me a million times.

"What did you say?" I ask hesitantly, to be sure my ears heard what my heart feels.

"I said I'm falling for you and, although I'm leaving next week, I want to take things to the next level with us. I'm talking about being exclusive. I've been thinking about relocating out here or, if worse comes to worse, you could kick it back home in LA with me."

He *is* saying what I think he's saying. All my life men shied away from that type of commitment with me, now here he's going into it with no pressure from me. I fall up against the wall and I slide down to the floor. I need to sit down but remember that Daffany doesn't have any furniture – not even a sofa. For one second, I feel bad for being so happy as I look around the apartment and see a world that, lately, has been coming to an end for her. But Cannon, waiting on my answer, makes me feel a little better.

"I'm falling for you too," I respond, needing him to know the feeling is mutual.

"Good," he says. I sense he's smiling. "But there's more. It seems like whenever I try to get closer to you and get to know you better, you push me away."

"That's not true, Cannon," I reply, hoping the pitch in my voice will convince him that I ain't trying to move away 'cuz I'm definitely trying to get closer to him. "Why you say that?"

"For one whenever I ask to meet your friends you tell me later. You don't like to talk about them or anything and I hate to rush things, Parade but I'm looking to be your man. And if I'm your man I need to know about *all* aspects of your life and for you to trust me."

"My life," I reiterate, loving the idea of me having one before he entered the picture. I must've done a good job of convincing him I'm someone other than Parade Knight.

"Yes, baby," he says. "I'm serious. But, what's up with you not letting me all the way in your life? I'm leaving next week and I want to meet everyone that's important to you." I can hear the frustration in his voice.

As Cannon's every word continues to make my dreams come true I feel terrible about keeping him away from that part of me. But I'm scared. I'm petrified about him finding out that I'm not the person I've presented to him. I'm worried about him finding out that all the designer things I wear were given to me because one of my best friends in the world cared enough to make sure I'm tight.

I don't want him to find out that a day before he met me I was nappy-headed and slept with my best friend's man just to be like her. But most of all, I don't want him to hear how badly she talks about me.

"I understand, Cannon and you're right." I hesitantly submit. "Well...we have a get together the last Friday of each month and if you want, you can meet them all then."

"I'd like that, Parade. This means a lot to me," he responds.

"And it means a lot to me that it means a lot to you." I laugh.

Suddenly, there is excessive knocking at the door. Cannon hears it and asks me if I will be okay since I told him what happened to Daffany. Maybe he doesn't want the same thing happening to me. But something tells me that the incident was related to her lifestyle so I feel that I don't have anything to worry about.

"I'm okay, Cannon. I'll call you back later."

"You sure?" he insists. "I can be in my car in a minute if something's up."

"I'll be okay. I'll talk to you later."

I walk to the door and trip out when I see Jay on the other side. *What the fuck?* I wonder how he knew I was here, but then I realize it isn't hard to find anything out around the Manor. I fix my hair a little without a mirror and open the door.

"Jay...what are you..."

Before I can say anything to him, he pushes his way in and closes the door behind me.

"What up, Parade? Why the fuck you dodging me?" He yells. "First you in my pockets and now whenever I call you, you can't be found."

"Where have I been? Come on, Jay. Why are you even talking to me like this?" I ask questioning if I should tell him I have somebody else in my life and that eventually whatever arrangement we have will come to an end.

"What?" he says as he squints his eyes and tilts his head. "I'm talking to you like that because I think you're trying to play me."

For real, all this shit Jay's doing is bullshit. *He* is the main one telling me not to fall in love with him. Now here he is in Daffany's apartment fussing at me like I'm his girlfriend or something. Maybe before Cannon came in my life I would've been excited about this but right now I'm not.

"Jay, I'm not your girlfriend and I've been meaning to talk to you about what we're doing anyway."

"What's up?"

"What we have together whatever it is, is gonna have to stop. I think Sky's suspecting something and I'm not cool with it no more. She's like my best friend."

"Are you kidding me, bitch? You get in my pockets for over $800 in the past few weeks and now you wanna cut me off? Fuck that shit."

"I'm sorry, Jay," I say with my hands in front of me, in case he acts stupid. "Look, I start a job next week. I'll pay back everything I got from you, I promise. It's just that...I love Sky and I don't want to sneak around with you no more. I want you two to work on your relationship."

"What you talking 'bout, Parade? We been fucking for over six months and now all of a sudden you got a conscience?"

"I've *been* conscious about what we're doing. Do you know she asked to use my phone one day from here to call you? Do you know that if I had let her use it, she would've seen your name pop up as Secret Lover? I'm tired of doing this shit, Jay. That was way too close for me. And lately she hasn't returned any of my calls. It wasn't until Daffany got hurt that I even seen her," I explain as he walked all the way into the apartment and begin to look around.

"Yeah, Sky called me and told me what happened and that's some fucked up shit," he continues as he stands in front of me. "I told Sky if she knew who did that shit I'd deal with that nigga for her. His ass would have made the list along with the mothafucka who raped my niece. But Sky said she ain't know who it was."

"Yeah...even if she did she wouldn't tell us," I respond and back away from him. "She don't like nobody knowing her business."

"Look," he says, walking up to me again and placing one of his arms around my waist. "I ain't trying to stop what we got right now. I think' I'm checking for you and that pussy curves to my dick." He smiles as if that will turn me on. "So we ain't cutting shit off till the fuck *I* say so."

"Oh, so what... you think me and Sky is suppose to be available to you whenever you want us to?" I pause waiting for his response. "Well I'm not fucking around with you no more. I want a man and family of my own someday and not one who doesn't belong to me."

"Why you lunching?" he asks as he walks away from me toward Daffany's window. I guess he's checking on his car or something. "Listen...kill that noise man 'cuz you've been taking my money so, as far as I'm concerned you belong to me. Unless you want me to tell her what we've been doing."

"Why would you do that? She'll be mad at you too, Jay."

"Man, I don't give a fuck. I cut her ass off the other day, anyway. I ain't even hear from her until she called about Daf."

"So you don't fuck with her no more? 'Cuz Miss Wayne told me he saw her get in your car last night."

"That's only 'cuz she pressing me. I ain't fucking with that girl for real."

"Oh! So, now that you through with her you'll ruin my friendship?"

"Like I said it ain't over till *I* say it's over."

I can't believe that calling it quits with Jay is harder on him than it is on me. He doesn't even care if Sky finds out about us but she wouldn't waste any time cutting me off. I wish I had never gotten involved with him.

"Just so you know, you can't make me fuck with you if I don't want to," I state as I look at him. "So even if you tell her that doesn't mean I'll be bothered with you."

"What I'm saying is this," he speaks real slowly. "This will end when the fuck I want it to end. Don't start changing on me just 'cuz you got your hair done and shit. It's my money that made it possible." He pauses and snatches my arm. "I ain't never had a black bitch cut me off before and I ain't starting now. You feel me, Parade?" He grabs my arm tighter.

"Yes," I reply and nod.

Now what? I don't know what he has planned for me. His phone rings. I know its Sky by his response. Thank God, who knows what he was about to do? All I

Black and Ugly

want is for this to be over and for him to move on. This is a mistake I'll never make again. Maybe I should just tell Sky the truth and get it over with myself.

"Look…I gotta go," he says breaking my train of thought, "but this conversation ain't over. If you fucking with some other cat get rid of his ass if you can't handle us both. I'm out." He drops several hundred dollars and walks out the door.

CHAPTER 25

SKY

Looking at Jay's car in front of Daffany's apartment building hurts like seeing another female rocking the same exclusive outfit. Why does he have to do this shit to me? We just got back together and I thought things were working out. I did everything he wanted me to do except get rid of my friends including the bitch who is trying to steal my man. And to think, I actually felt bad for dissing her lately. That was my whole reason for going over her house but when her mother told me she was at Miss Wayne's I went there.

He was the one who told me she's cleaning Daffany's apartment for her, again. I think they are doing an awful lot for somebody who got beat up because she's a whore. Everything she got is partially her fault. But seeing my boyfriend's car makes me hate everything and everybody. Now I'm getting ready to fuck him up.

"You want me to go with you?" Jewel asks.

"No. Wait in the car."

I don't want Jewel hearing or seeing whatever is getting ready to happen. The only reason she's with me is because she popped over my house when I was looking for Parade. But now as I see my boyfriend's white Yukon sitting outside Daffany's apartment I can no longer hide the tears if I want to.

So, I told Jewel almost everything, like how he's probably been fucking with her for the past five months right under my fucking nose. Even though I wish I never invited her along she made me feel better by saying if he wanted to fuck with a hood rat then he doesn't deserve me anyway. And she's right. But it doesn't change the fact, that for once in life it will look like Parade got the best of me.

I get out the car and walk up to the building. I want to catch him in Daffany's apartment but he's coming down the steps in the hallway.

"What you doing here, Jay!? Why you ain't answer your phone?"

His eyes grow wide and I know I've caught his no-good ass red handed. He probably came out looking for my car 'cuz I called him. But I parked on the side of the building so he wouldn't see me.

"There you go," he says all loud. "I been looking for you."

"You been looking for me? No the fuck you ain't been looking for me either. The only thing you been looking for was Parade's black ass."

"Why you gotta be all loud and shit in the hallway?" he responds trying to intimidate me.

But it doesn't work. All I can think about is that he's embarrassed me and now Jewel will know that my man chose a dusty bitch over me. Plus I can't talk low if I want to. He's carried me.

"Why I gotta be loud? Why the fuck I gotta be loud? I gotta be loud cuz you cheating on me with Parade, Jay. I would've never pegged you for a dirty nigga. Do you realize how many dudes want to be with me that I passed up fucking with you, Jay?"

He's quiet but the look he gives me doesn't look like guilt. He looks like he has something else on his mind that I don't know anything about.

"You gonna feel real stupid after this shit, Sky. Real fucking stupid."

"What you talking about, Jay? How the fuck I'm gonna feel stupid when you the one sleeping with my best friend?"

"You gonna feel real stupid because you got shit all wrong that's why."

"All wrong? What you talking about, Jay? Have you or have you not been sneaking behind my back seeing Parade for the past few months?"

"Yes," he says but his answer catches me off guard and I hold on to the rail for support.

"Yes?" I ask him, trying to give him a chance to explain. "What do you mean *yes*, Jay? You don't even feel bad about this?"

"No I don't. I'm tired of you not trusting me, Sky. And I'm tired of you throwing niggas in my face. You think just 'cuz I like light-skin chicks that you can treat me like I'm a pussy-ass nigga. Yeah I fucks with the red broads but you ain't the only light-skin chick in the world, Sky. You just the one I chose."

I'm crying so hard that I can barely see him.

"You bitch. You fucking bitch. I can't believe I wasted all my time on you," I scream as I repeatedly beat his chest with my fists. "How could you do this to me?"

"I could do this to you 'cuz I love you."

"What?" I say. "'Cuz you love me? Jay, what in the fuck are you talking about?"

"I'm saying I've been keeping time with Parade but it's not for the reasons you think it is. It's 'cuz you told me she was your friend even though I ain't want you fucking with her. And, I needed somebody to help me pick out the right ring for the woman I want to marry. I figured only your best friend could really know what you want. And she was gonna help me with the proposal."

"What?" I question, instantly feeling happiness in place of sadness. "What did you say?"

"I said that Parade has been helping me plan how I was gonna propose to you."

"Oh, Jay," I whisper as I jump up and hug him. "Baby, I'm so sorry. Please forgive me." I kiss him all over his face. "I didn't mess things up did I? Do you realize how happy this makes me? I knew you couldn't be attracted to Parade over me. I knew it but I needed to hear it from you."

"Come on, man. Why would I fuck with Parade? You know how I feel about dark chicks."

"I know, baby but she was acting weird and I smelled the perfume I gave her on your clothes...and I'm so sorry," I explain, talking in circles. "This explains everything."

I'm relieved. I'm so fucking relieved that Jay ain't ready to leave me to be with Parade.

"Now how you feel?" he asks as he smiles at me and pulls me to him. "You acting all jealous and shit and now you fucked up everything. I'da never thought you would think Parade is any competition for you. Damn, ma."

Now I'm embarrassed. I made a fool out of myself and he'll always think that I thought Parade was in my league. I have to think of something. I can't live with him thinking that because I don't care how she looks now she will never have nothing on me.

"Boy never did I think she's any competition. You must've lost your mind." I laugh. "It's just that Parade ain't the person you think she is and lately my mind has been messed up. That's all."

"What you mean?" he asks.

"I mean Parade did something to somebody real fucked up and ever since it happened it's messed my head up about her. She not the person I thought she was."

"What you talking 'bout, shawty? If you gonna tell me, tell me the whole story."

"I can't go into detail right now. Let's just say she has a lot to do with what happened at the party the night that girl was killed and leave it at that."

He backs up looks at me then laughs. It pisses me off that he doesn't believe me.

"Yeah, 'aight. Whatever you say. If you feel like she's competition, you feel like she's competition. It's okay. I'm a handsome dude and you got a little jealous that's all," he adds as he playfully punches my face. "But if you care anything about shawty you really shouldn't go around making shit like that up. Parade can get fucked up because that bitch was a major ballers wife."

"I ain't making shit up. So what you don't believe me?" I ask while feeling more embarrassed that I told him anything.

"No, I don't."

"Well, why should I believe anything you just told me then? I mean you just told me you came out of the apartment because she was helping you propose to me right? So why don't I ask her just to make sure since we not believing each other around here," I propose as I take one step closer to Daffany's door.

The sly smile he had on his face a few seconds ago is wiped off. Yeah, mothafucka I got you.

"Why you acting stupid? Let's go," he says as he pulls my arm.

"No," I say as I snatch it back. "I ain't going nowhere. I'm gonna ask her right fucking now if what you telling me is true."

"You know what if you gonna act like that it's over," he responds as he walks out the building door.

I know exactly what he's doing. He wants me to be all scared to lose him and go running behind him and shit but I want him to be as embarrassed and fucked up as he just made me feel. And I want to make sure what he's saying is true.

The moment I knock on the door Jay comes back in and runs up behind me.

"Don't do this shit, Sky. Why you fucking with that girl?" he yells.

I don't say anything just knock. Parade finally opens and I hate how cute she looks. Her hair is still

Black and Ugly

new and she has on a cute Baby Phat one-piece cat suit. Even her makeup looks nice but I can tell it isn't MAC.

It seems like the more days that go by the better she appears. Any other time, when we didn't talk for a while she'd fall off but lately that ain't the case. And, that makes me hate her even more.

"Hey, Sky," she says excited to see me. "What you doing here?"

"I need to know something right now."

"You wanna come in? I'm just cleaning Daffany's apartment since she's still having trouble moving around. Me and Miss Wayne ordered her a new living room set and it'll be coming later."

"Well that's good for Daffany," I reply unenthused about what they're doing for her.

The three of them did more stuff for one another than they did for me. But it's to be expected because they have always been jealous of me. I bet you Parade paid the same thing for that cat suit that she paid for the purse Miss Wayne gave her, nothing.

"Well what's up?" she asks as the smile is removed from her face. "What you got to talk to me about?" She looks at Jay and back at me.

"What was Jay doing over here just now?"

"I told you…" Jay interrupts.

"Shut the fuck up, Jay. I'm talking to Parade," I snap as I throw my hand up so the back of it is in his face.

"Man, fuck this shit," he yells and walks out the building. "I'm outta here."

Everything he just did proves his guilt even more. If he ain't have nothing to worry about, why he run back in the building?

"I don't think I should tell you, Sky."

"Why not, bitch? Why don't you think you should fucking tell me?"

She instantly looks like she is on the verge of crying. She never could take it when I call her out her name and I smile inside because I know I can still control her feelings no matter what. Maybe now that smile can be wiped off her face with the cheap makeup she's wearing.

"I can't tell you," she states in a low voice while looking down, "cuz it'll ruin Jay's marriage proposal to you." She gently closes the door.

As I stand in the hallway facing Daffany's door, an immediate feeling of embarrassment and loss takes over me. I'm sure that after today I have lost Jay for good. All I want to do is run and hide but I know that the moment I get in the car Jewel will be waiting to hear the details.

Damn.

CHAPTER 26

MARKEE

"Markee, you gonna have to chill the fuck out, man. You don't have to shoot every mothafucka you have a run in with. Now, you being trigger happy is fucking making shit hot for the rest of us."

Markee listens to his older brother, Silver. But for real he isn't feeling him. He's tired of people treating him like he's a kid and feels he has to step up his game to prove himself more. He can't count the number of times a nigga on the block laughed in his face when he was about to stick them up, that is until he pulled the trigger.

"Sil, that nigga tried to play me. He gonna holla 'bout he wasn't giving me shit and to do what I have to do. So what the fuck? I pulled the trigger eight fucking times," Markee shoots back.

"First off, little nigga," Silver says with irritation in his voice. "I didn't give you the order to hit Kwame's block. You don't do a mothafucking thing without running it past me first."

"I did run it past you. And what you tell me? Chill the fuck out until shit cools off from the other spots I stuck up. But shit was nice and cool when I got there so I took that nigga out."

Silver's reminding Markee of how old he is gets to him. *How many mothafuckas do I have to kill until he respects me?* Markee wonders. He's tired of standing by waiting on orders when shit needs to be done but until he earns the respect of his older brother and cousins he's gonna have to rely on niggas from his original home, Baltimore to hold shit down with him.

"Listen, Markee," Silver says as he breathes so heavily in the phone due to being angry that his feelings closely resemble hate. "Now you gonna chill the fuck out and don't make no other moves 'till I fucking tell you to. There's some other shit that's getting ready to go down with Sky and her girls and I don't want the heat from their bodies falling on us, too. So I'm not asking you, mothafucka I'm *telling* you to chill the fuck out. What I got to do, get a stroller and strap you in like you a mothafucking kid?"

Silver pauses for a minute and focuses on his brother's heavy sighing. He immediately knows that he's beyond mad but he doesn't care. Between slapping women for stupid shit and raping girls around the way Markee is turning up too much unnecessary heat.

At first Silver let the little shit slide but now he has to address him. Whenever something went down in

Black and Ugly

the Manor no matter who else in the family did it, it was always blamed on Silver and them. Nobody ever ran around saying, "Markee and them," because it was Silver who built the reputation for the family when he was Markee's age.

"And just so you know, *big bruh*, I don't think Eclipse is gonna do shit but fuck them bitches. He be riding around with Parade like she his bitch. If we wait on this mothafucka to do what gotta be done we won't never make no money."

"Like I said, chill out and don't make no more moves. Do I make myself clear?" Silver yells.

He doesn't get a response so he yells again, "DO I MAKE MYSELF CLEAR?"

"Yeah, big bruh. You make yourself clear," he answers as he hangs up the phone with complete disregard to everything his brother just said.

CHAPTER 27

PARADE

"Miss Wayne, I'm coming in a minute. And don't worry, I'll be fine."

"I know you will," he whispers as to not wake up Daffany who just fell asleep on his couch. "But, it's dark now and I don't like you walking by yourself."

"I know, daddy but I'll be fine," I say, sensing how much he cares about me. "I was just adding the finishing touches on Daffany's apartment. She's been so stressed out that I want things to be as nice as possible for her when she comes home tomorrow."

"Okay," he says and sighs. "And how are you feeling about that other thing that happened?"

"You mean with Sky?" I ask, already knowing what he's talking about but wanting to avoid it.

"Now, you know I'm talking 'bout that dry pussy bitch so stop playing with me."

"I know you are." I laugh.

"Well...how are you holding up with her coming to the door questioning you about Jay's slutty ass?"

"I'm fine," I say even though I'm not.

Hearing how Sky really feels about me due to my listening to them in the hallway hurts a lot. But, at the

208   *Black and Ugly*

same time I am wrong for sleeping with her man. Yet she talked about me like she's never cared, even before suspecting anything ever happened between Jay and me. But for some reason I always loved Sky.

"Did his double dipping ass call you yet?"

"Yes, he did. I told him that she didn't know anything and I was able to confirm his story because I overheard them. I also let him know I can't see him anymore 'cuz I hate sneaking around behind Sky's back anyway."

"Will he let you go that easy?" he asks, remembering the threats I told him Jay made earlier.

"I hope so. Maybe, since we almost got caught he'll realize it's not worth it."

"My baby done turned into a black Barbie doll and now everybody wants her." He laughs.

"Stop playing. You know that's not true," I say trying not to blush.

"Honey, sooner or later, you gonna realize that you have always been beautiful. It's just that now you're starting to show it," he explains in a loving voice. "And I think it's for the best that you leave him alone too. After that little stunt Sky pulled by asking to use your cell phone, she's liable to do anything to catch you two. And any-who, you have a new man. Speaking of such when you bringing him by to meet me and Daffany?"

"Well...he has been wanting to meet you so I'll be bringing him to our end-of-the-month get-together."

"Oh, *really?*" Miss Wayne says. "What you do? Tell him how beautiful I was?"

"No." I laugh. "I told him how much I love you. But I'll tell him how beautiful you are later."

"Parade, you don't know how good that makes me feel to hear you love me. It's one thing to know someone loves you but it's a whole 'notha thing to hear them say it."

"Well...let me get off this phone before you get all teary eyed and shit," I tell him.

"Yes girl, 'cuz you know I'm getting ready to get juicy eyed.'"

"Bye, boy," I say. "And just so you know the furniture is beautiful. Do you think the person who beat her, stole her things too?"

"Probably so," Miss Wayne responds. "But who truly knows? Miss Sky was the last person to see her place intact with the exception of the bastard who hurt her."

"You don't think she had anything to do with it, do you?" I ask, wondering if he suspects Sky is a little untrustworthy too.

"Let me just say this. I've known Sky all my life only to realize that I don't know her very much at all. Now hurry up home. Dinner is getting cold."

Black and Ugly

I get off the phone and wonder what he means. But after thinking of the things I heard Sky say about me in the hall I have other issues on my mind.

BANG, BANG, BANG.

Why do black people have to knock on doors so hard? I wonder. I hope it isn't the same man who hurt Daffany. One thing's for sure I ain't opening up shit unless I feel it's okay.

I look out the peephole and see it's Cliff from next door. He's always so sweet and his wife is beautiful. He helped the movers bring all Daffany's furniture in earlier. When I first asked him to lend a hand he looked kinda strange but when he saw everything Miss Wayne and I had he agreed.

I open the door thinking he left something.

"Hey, Cliff. You leave something?" I ask.

"No," he says. "I was coming to see how everything turned out."

"Well, don't stand out in the hallway, boy. Get in," I yell as I grab him by the arm and lock the door. "I don't like talking with the door open after what happened to Daffany. This neighborhood has gotten worse over the years."

"Yeah. It has," he responds coldly clearly in a different mood than he was in earlier.

He goes through the kitchen her bedroom and the bathroom and then comes back in the living room.

"Everything looks real nice," he says. "So when she coming home?"

"Tomorrow," I answer with a smile. "You think she'll like it?"

"I don't know," Cliff utters as if he's mad. "It looks even better than before." He looks at me with a glassy expression in his eyes.

I realize he's drunk. Suddenly, I feel stupid for letting him in Daffany's apartment without her permission. Now if he wants to he can steal everything in here because he knows where it is.

"Okay," I say trying to push him out. "Let me finish up here." I slightly open the door.

"Did I tell you how good you been looking lately, Parade? You been looking really fucking good," he continues as he slams the door shut with one hand and pushes me away with the other. "Damn, that outfit you wearing is making my dick hard." He grabs it. "I wonder what's in it. I wonder if your pussy is as pink and soft as it looks pressed up between your thick, pretty legs. You gonna let me get in that pussy, Parade?"

Oh my goodness! I'm getting ready to be raped! I could have never seen this coming. And now, here in Daffany's apartment I'm getting ready to get raped by someone I trusted a man I've always looked up to and considered a good husband.

"Stop playing, Cliff," I state, attempting to make light of his actions. "I have to finish up around here."

"Who said I'm playing?" he responds. "Can you suck a dick as good as your friend? 'Cuz I'm getting ready to find out," he continues moving toward me.

"Please don't do this," I beg him. "Please don't do this to me." Each plea appears to bring him closer.

"Yeah. Keep begging, bitch. But I'm gonna give this shit to everybody she loves like she did to everyone I love."

I don't understand what he means, but I do know that he's drunk and has all intentions of raping me.

Suddenly I put things into perspective. Number one from what I could see it doesn't look like he has anything on him. Secondly I decide that the only way he's raping me will be on top of my cold dead body.

I continue to back away from him until we end up in Daffany's room.

"Now, where you gonna go you pretty chocolate bitch? It's been a long time since I tasted chocolate. And if I knew you were that sexy I would've fucked you a long time ago. If you don't fight it I won't put you in the hospital like I did that bitch!"

Oh God no! It was him. He was the one who beat Daffany. But what does he want to give to me that she gave to people he love? Before I could think about it anymore, he runs after me. I quickly open the closet door and grab the metal bat I bought for Daffany to keep in her room. It was supposed to be for protection and although it wouldn't stop a bullet it was all I could afford.

With one quick movement, I swing at his head and he stumbles but remains on his feet. His eyes are now wide open and he looks crazed but more conscious than he was before. *Yeah, you ain't drunk no more, mothafucka now are you?*

I can tell he wasn't expecting me to fight back so he goes for the door. Something comes over me and I don't know what it is but I run and knock him upside his fucking head again.

"Hold up what are you doing?" he continues with his hands up.

"I'm whooping your ass," I respond hitting him again.

"Can you please stop hitting me?" he pleads with his hands up as if they would block my blows. "I was just playing with you." He screams in pain.

He tries to grab the bat as if he can take it. But little did he know I'm a pro with a bat having used it on more than one occasion to handle bitches trying to jump me.

Suddenly I blank out and can't hear a word he's saying. All I could think about was my sister lying up in the hospital bed and how I know he is to blame.

214   *Black and Ugly*

Daffany didn't deserve any of the shit he did to her. I don't care what he's talking about.

"Parade...pllleasse. Let me leave. I just wanna go home."

"Fuck you, mothafucka. You should have thought about that before you tried your hand. Since you like to rape girls I'm gonna keep kicking your fucking ass till I get tired. And the next time you think about hurting Daffany I want you to remember this beat down." I knock him in his head again.

By the time I finished punishing him for what he did to Daffany and was trying to do to me he's spread out on the kitchen floor, unconscious.

I hit him one last time to make sure he won't move then pick up Daffany's home phone to make a call. "This is Parade Knight and I'd like to report a break-in but there's no rush, ma'am. I have everything under control here."

CHAPTER 28

DAFFANY

Waking up this morning is nice until I hear about what happened to Parade last night. And the moment they gave me the details I was filled with guilt. I would've taken it really hard if he had succeeded at raping her. And for the first time ever I'm starting to think that it wasn't a good idea to conceal *everything* about my lifestyle from my friends. If I would have told them that it was Cliff who beat me then Parade would've never trusted him and opened the door.

We are sitting on the couch discussing the details and Miss Wayne says, "Daffany, I'm happy you agreed to press charges with Parade after all, honey. And don't even worry about him. They're keeping an eye on his tired ass."

"I know," I respond with my head hung low, "but I'm so sorry about what almost happened to Parade."

"Don't worry about it, girl. It ain't your damn fault," Parade insists as she moves closer to me. "He's the one who should be sorry. He's gonna be locked up the moment he comes out of ICU. Believe that."

"Did you beat him that bad, girl?" Miss Wayne asks, laughing.

"I beat him silly," she says as she gives Miss Wayne a high five.

"I bet you did." I manage to smile. "But there's something else you don't know that I have to tell you," I continue as I start crying.

"What? What's wrong?" Miss Wayne asks as he kneels in front of me while I'm sitting on his couch. "I have to tell Parade that I know what he meant when he said that he wanted to give her what I gave his loved ones."

"You...do?" Parade stutters.

"Yes," I whisper.

"What?" Parade responds real slowly. "Because I thought he was on that shit and was talking out of his head."

"Please forgive me," I ask as it becomes harder to release a secret that I had planned to take to my grave. "I didn't know that this was gonna happen or I would've told you before."

Parade and Miss Wayne look at each other as they could sense that whatever I'm getting ready to tell them is pretty serious. But the phone rings before I can release the words to inform them that I'm HIV positive.

"Go ahead, baby. Whoever that is can wait," Miss Wayne informs me.

"No...please answer the phone. I'll tell you when you're done," I insist feeling relieved that I have a few more seconds to prolong.

"Can I get you something to drink?" Parade asks as she rubs my back.

"No. I'm okay," I say ear hustling to see what Miss Wayne is talking about.

Miss Wayne's phone conversation gets heated and I can tell that my announcement would have to be put off even longer which I don't mind.

"So what did you tell them, Miss Rick?" he yells into the phone. "But why would you use the card again after I told you not to? Well that doesn't make any since." He paces the floor and Parade runs to his side. "If you think I'm gonna get your black ass out of jail after I told you not to use that card you got another thing coming. Well fuck you too," he screams as he hangs up the phone.

Miss Wayne stands in the kitchen for a minute looking at the phone and fanning himself with his hand. I can tell that whatever just happened isn't good. He walks over to the couch, sits down and is trying to regain his composure. Parade follows him.

"What happened?" Parade asks. "Is everything okay with Miss Rick?"

218   *Black and Ugly*

"Hell no," he yells. "Girl...I told his ass not to use the card again after he got the last things. He goes and uses it behind my back and of course it was reported stolen. I should have took it away from his simple ass."

"Damn. I thought you told me he brought the stuff he wanted the last time he had the card," Parade questions.

"He did, girl. But *she's* a greedy bitch. So now, they have his ass up in jail looking like a fucking idiot. I'm so mad ya'll I don't know what to do." He pauses as he puts his face in his hands. "And then on top of everything he has the nerve to ask me to bail his dumb ass out. Do I look like a fucking fool?" he continues while switching his hands from the air to his hips.

"Damn. You think he gonna say something?" I ask.

"I don't know, chile. Hopefully he'll chill out and not open his mouth. Who knows?" he responds. He puts his hand on my leg acknowledging that he hasn't forgotten about me.

"Well...we'll have to keep our fingers crossed because you know Miss Rick runs his mouth like a bitch," Parade adds.

"And that ain't the only thing he running," he retorts as his voice gets lower. "I almost forgot until he called. But he's been sleeping with Cliff for the longest and the worse part is this he's HIV positive."

I'm in the room, but it's spinning around. I feel like a superhero is rotating the couch on his fingertip and wouldn't stop. I can't believe that the man terrorizing my friend and me, got HIV from someone else another man at that.

"Are you kidding me?" Parade yells as she jumps up. "That mothafucka probably got AIDS and was getting ready to give it to me," she continues as she paces the room.

"I know, girl but Miss Rick definitely has HIV," Miss Wayne says. "I told him the moment he found out to start using protection with that man. I wouldn't be surprised if he does have it."

At this point, they must realize if Miss Rick has it and possibly gave it to Cliff that I may have it too since I admitted to sleeping with him. But, I ain't ready to talk about it. I feel violated in the worse way possible. I always thought before he beat me up that Cliff was a good man who just needed something from me that he couldn't get from his wife. In a way I thought I was doing their marriage a favor by being with him because of the things we talked about. But now I'm finding out that nothing he has ever said to me was true. How could it be? If he cheated on his wife why wouldn't he lie to me? My head is thumping so hard that I can barely move it.

The phone rings and Miss Wayne runs to answer it again. I'm relieved because I no longer want to discuss what's up with me. I'm still taking in that I may have found out who gave this shit to me.

"She did what? What in the world is going on around here?" he yells apparently receiving more bad news. "I'll tell her, Ma. She's here anyway. Talk to you later," he continues as he ends the call and sits back on the couch.

"Daffany, that was my mother," he says, looking at me real concerned. "She said that Aunt Diana tried to sell a few of your things to people around the way including your TV. I'm so sorry, baby." He places one hand on my leg.

Parade covers her mouth as if she can't believe it. I sit here for a few seconds then decide I have to get out. I have to take a walk, otherwise I'm gonna jump out that window. It's like my world is not crumbling down around me but trying to crush me within it. I realize my mother is on drugs but I can't believe she stole everything I owned. All my possessions. I was so sure that Cliff stole my things that I didn't stop to consider anyone else. But out of all the things she took from me I don't understand why she would take the papers confirming my HIV status.

"I gotta go, ya'll," I say as I stand. "I have to go."

"Daffany, wait," Parade yells.

I don't stop. I'm out the door.

CHAPTER 29

SMOKES

"I'm hearing things, man," Smokes says to Eclipse on the phone while getting a back massage in his $700,000 home in Virginia. "I'm hearing things I don't like."

"Like what?" Eclipse asks growing frustrated at the interference in how he handles business.

"Folks telling me you joy riding in the fucking neighborhood instead of doing what needs to be done. Now I ain't got shit to do with you fucking shawty since I'm hearing she done came up and shit but how long you intend on stretching shit out?"

"What folks? Silver? He can't possibly tell you what I been doing because I don't discuss my business with nobody. Just because I don't choose to catch 'em on the corner and blaze them all doesn't mean I'm not working."

"I'm starting to think the blazing idea ain't too bad," Smokes says.

"Well give me half my money for the work I put in and do it yourself," Eclipse shoots back.

Smokes throws his hand up signaling the massage therapist to leave the room. She's gone and he continues, "Let me tell you something, dawg. I don't know who the fuck you think you talking to but you ain't running shit up here. That shit may fly in Texas but around here it'll get you killed. Now, I entrusted you to take care of the mothafucka who killed my wife. And as a result, I got a right to ask fucking questions."

"And I'm not saying you don't have a right. What I'm telling you is that I've learned from being in this business for years that a trigger-happy nigga leaves trails. By the time I finish with Parade and her friends I will be for certain that I got the right person with no exceptions and nothing leading to you. Let's not forget the only person who claimed she and her friends had something to do with it was Silver. We need to be sure."

"I understand this. But your tab is at fifteen mothafucking thousand including bullshit ass expenses. At this point, I want somebody dead even if they didn't do it. Do you know that whoever this mothafucka is took her jewelry? So I have concerns about them trying to play me. I want shit done."

"And I got that."

"Well hurry the fuck up," Smokes commands.

Smokes is upset at hearing from Silver that Eclipse is cruising around with Parade at his expense. Even though Eclipse told him he works slowly he's embarrassed by the idea of him spending his money and everybody knowing it.

"Like I said," Eclipse continues calmly understanding Smokes' frustrations, "I handle my business differently than Silver and the rest of them dudes you've dealt with. Let's not forget you called me from Texas. Now I thought you hired me because you wanted shit done right."

"And I do but..."

"Then let me handle my job," he interrupts. "Parade ain't like the other females I met. She seems loyal to her friends and, even though I've succeeded at convincing her that I care about her she ain't saying shit. As a matter of fact I'm sure she didn't have anything to do with what happened to your wife. I don't know about the others but she's introducing me to the rest of them tomorrow. And if I don't get the answer I want from somebody, I'm killing everybody."

"That's what I want to hear," Smokes says and hangs up the phone.

CHAPTER 30

SKY

"I didn't know ya'll still wanted me to come."

"Why wouldn't we, Miss Sky? Stop acting like that," Miss Wayne says.

"Did you tell Parade and Daffany I'm coming?" I ask.

"Miss Sky, we've been friends damn near all our lives. And no matter what we've always gotten together on the last Friday of every month."

"And your point?" I question.

"And my point is, Miss Smarty-pants that I wouldn't have to tell them anything because we've always expected you to be there. And Miss Parade is bringing over her new boyfriend so I figured you'd want to meet him."

The moment he says that I know I have to be there. I want to show her exactly how quickly a man can lose focus. I'll be doing her a favor. There's no reason for her getting too attached. It'll never last anyway. And even though Jay isn't fucking with her I want her to see that most men will stray.

"Of course I'll be there, baby," I say happily.

"Okay," he responds, wondering what gave me a change of heart.

"Well let me go and throw something on."

"Bye, chile," he says and he hangs up.

The first thing I go for is my black Donna Karan dress that I will dress down a little with my custom-made jean jacket. I also grab my jewelry and jump in the shower.

Once out of the shower I call Jay to cancel our plans for the night because I have no intentions on meeting him like I originally desired. My plans were to show him how sorry I was for not trusting him but I can do that tomorrow.

"Hey, baby."

"Yeah." He pauses. "What?" he says real coldly.

"What's wrong with you?" I ask trying to soften him up.

"Nothing. We still on tonight or what?"

I can definitely tell that he wants to get straight to the point.

"Actually that's what I want to talk to you about. I forgot our monthly thing is tonight so I won't be able to come."

"I thought you said you ain't fuck with them for whatever reason."

"I did but I realize I miss them now."

"Yeah...whatever. Look. About us...I ain't fucking with you no more. I was gonna tell you straight up tonight but since we ain't meeting I can tell you over the phone."

I sit down on the sofa and ask him to repeat what he just said to me.

"I don't understand, Jay," I say scared he'd say the same thing. "Why are you doing this?"

"'Cuz, Shawty I'm tired of your reckless mouth. You act like a fucking kid. That shit you pulled the other day was bullshit. You played yourself."

"Baby, please don't do this to me. Don't do this to us," I plead as I try not to beg but convince him that I need him.

"Listen, you been crowding my style for a while now. So for real it was just a matter of time before I cut you off. Don't take it bad. What we had was cool while it lasted."

"I been crowding your style for how long, Jay?" I inquire as I start to get mad. "I mean, how long have you felt this way?"

"For the past year. I've been wanting to cut you off for a minute but I felt sorry for you. I just ain't know how to say it. Plus I didn't feel like hearing your fucking mouth."

"So if that's the case you never had any intentions on marrying me did you?"

Silence.

"Listen it just ain't working 'aight?" he continues in a low voice.

"Jay," I say as I brace myself for this question, "is it because of Parade?"

"Yeah I wish," he answers with a laugh. "Shawty stopped taking my calls ever since you did that shit to her. She ain't having nothing else to do with me."

I'm trying to calm down but he just admitted to sleeping with my friend and wanting her and not me. My world is slipping from underneath me.

"Hey, baby," my moms says as she comes from her bedroom. "How you like this ad me and your father did for Sean John last weekend? It just printed today."

"Not right now, Ma," I respond as I look up at her from the floor.

"Okay," she says, seeing my tears but leaving the room.

I need to be alone while I do something I never did - beg a man to stay, beg him to give me another chance and pray that he will.

"Is there anything," I ask real slowly, "*anything* at all that I can do to make you stay with me? I can be everything she was to you, baby. I know I have a problem with my mouth sometimes. I can work on that for you. Just don't do this."

"Naw, man. It's over," he insists and ends the call.

I run into my room and immediately start crying. Who's gonna take care of me now? I spent so much time with Jay lately that I haven't even pursued anybody else. I hate that fucking bitch. She backstabbed me in the worst way this time. And now she can have Jay anytime she wants.

I don't understand. I can't understand. What did she do that's so fucking special? Just a few weeks ago she couldn't even dress. I bet he was giving her money too. Maybe Miss Wayne's in on it as well. Probably Daffany too. I can't stand none of them. They were probably laughing behind my back the whole time.

I reach under my bed to grab the photo album of me, Miss Wayne, Daffany and Parade and rip up all the pictures. I finally realize that the only person I have in this world is me. I kick off my shoes, lie on my bed and cry my eyes out like there's no tomorrow.

CHAPTER 31

DAFFANY

"Just tell me the truth, Mamma. It's not like everybody don't know already. Do you know how embarrassing this is?" I say as I lean up against the bare wall in her apartment while she continues to pace the floor.

She has not one picture of me in her place and I'm her only child. This place is as ugly and as gloomy as it was when I left it.

"I don't know what you talking about, Daffany," my mother answers as she continuously rubs her arms, *typical crackhead behavior.* "They lying on me."

"Ma," I say, trying not to be upset, "I don't care about my stuff no more. My friends brought me all new things. I just need to know why you stole from me. That's all I wanna know." I slump down on her mattress on the living room floor.

She looks at me and tries to touch me. I pull away not wanting to have any feelings for a woman who cares only for herself. All my life she's been addicted to someone or something. First it was men, then coke and now, it's crack. I always had to fend for myself or I would've had nothing. And on many nights I had to take care of her too.

"Baby, I'm sorry. When Sky came and got me to look after the apartment while you were in the hospital," she said continuously moving around, "I lost it."

The idea of Sky getting her to watch my place bothers me. Sky knows my mother can't be trusted with a butter knife let alone a fully furnished apartment. I try my hardest not to think that she did it on purpose but I'm starting to believe she's just that conniving.

"I tried to do what she wanted me to, baby," she continues, "but this shit got me all fucked up, real fucked up in the head, Daffany. And I thought if I invited a few people over to take a few things they'll give me some money and that you wouldn't notice."

"That I wouldn't notice? Are you that gone, Mamma? Why wouldn't I fucking notice?" I scream.

"I mean…I thought it would be okay. But then they started taking everything…I told them not to touch your clothes and stuff but they took them too."

"So you had strangers in my house?" I ask, internalizing the concept of people entering my home to steal my things with my mother's help. "Do you realize how bad you make me look?"

"I'm sorry, baby," she says as she tries to touch my left arm but I snatch it back.

"Who was it, Mamma? Who came in my place and stole my things? Huh? I don't want them back. I just gotta know who witnessed a mother stealing from her daughter," I continue then stand.

"It was a bunch of people," she says with her head hanging low.

"A bunch of people like who, Mamma? Who came in my fucking house? I deserve for you to at least tell me that," I yell.

"Umm...that little boy Marcus and ummmm, Karen ...and her oldest son Keith. And ummmmm...the rest I can't remember. I'm sorry, Daffany and I want you to know this is it for me. I ain't fucking with that shit no more. That shit has made me steal from my baby. This is it for real. I'm gonna be a real mother to you wait and see."

I look at my mother with disgust and pity. I can no longer count the number of times she said that to me. And I know that little boy Marcus she's talking about is nobody else but Markee. I'm afraid - afraid that she will not know the answer to the biggest question I have to ask her. It's now obvious that she did this for profit so what happened to the papers. They couldn't benefit her or any of them other rogues. Still, I have to ask.

"Mamma, there were some very important papers under the bed. Where are they?" I question as I gently grab her arms and look at her face, a once beautiful face but now it resembles one of a 59-year-old woman instead of a 39-year-old.

She starts to scratch her hair then her arms. I can tell she is really thinking but 15 years of smoking crack has taken its toll. I decide to leave after realizing she doesn't know anything and if she did she can't remember.

"Never mind, Mamma," I say as I head for the door then walk out.

"I'm sorry, baby. I'm so sorry."

CHAPTER 32

SKY

Despite what happened, I decide to come anyway. There is no way I will allow her to steal my man without a chance at stealing hers too. I've been looking at him all night and I have a feeling he wants me. They always do.

"So Parade tells me you live around here too," he asks.

"Yes, Cannon," I answer seductively with a smile. "I've been living around here all my life."

"It must be nice to have friends in your life you've known for so long," he continues as I turn to look at Miss Wayne and Parade who are still in the kitchen. I roll my eyes.

"It's okay... *I guess.*"

"Oh really?" he says, detecting something in my voice. "I'm gonna leave that one alone."

Oh! I feel we are starting to connect. Damn! The bitch calls me from the kitchen.

"Sky! Did you want anything? We gonna start the game when Daffany gets here."

Yes, bitch. I would like my man back. Can you do that? I wonder.

But instead I say, "No thank you, *very good friend.*" I give them both my super fake ass smile, the one that I had reserved for Jay's niece.

I notice that Cannon appear to be staring at me but not like he wants me more like he's trying to understand me.

"Is everything okay?" I ask trying to feel him out.

"Yeah. Everything's cool."

Just then, Parade and Miss Wayne come out the kitchen holding a tray with a bunch of snacks - pigs in the blanket, cheese and crackers, potato chips and potato salad. I've never understood what's up with him and potato salad. He eat that shit everyday.

"Here you go ladies and gentlemen," he says in his usual gay manner. "Dinner is served."

He's wearing a red spaghetti-strapped dress with his fuzzy red slippers since we're not going out and I think he looks ridiculous. If I was Parade I would be embarrassed but the two of them appear to be in another world. Her hair looks freshly done so I can tell it's new. This time she has soft curls throughout her head and is wearing a Calvin Klein skirt set with a fresh pair of tennis. Once again, she has a new bag and this one is by Marc Jacobs. Out of anger I drop three pigs in a blanket on the floor. But they don't stain. Damn!

I decide that at that moment her man isn't paying enough attention to me so I remove my jean jacket, stand then flaunt the form-fitting Donna Karan dress as if I on a runway.

"What you doing girl? Giving us a fashion show?" Miss Wayne laughs.

"No," I respond, feeling embarrassed. "I'm just going to get something to drink."

"Damn it I did forget the drinks didn't I? Honey chile, bring me something too. I want a Coke," Miss Wayne yells. "And what ya'll want?" he asks Parade and Cannon who appear to be on their on planet with all the kissing. "I want Coke, too, Sky. And what you want, baby?" she asks as she reaches in for another kiss. He accepts.

"Nothing," he snaps staring at me like he is looking straight through me instead of at me.

I hate them bitches. Trying to carry me in front of company. Any other time Parade would be waiting on me.

I grab two glasses, move out of their view from the living room turn around and dig my hands between my legs. Then I stick my finger in my pussy and smear it on the inside of Miss Wayne and Parade's glasses.

I'm getting ready to pour the soda. I turn back around and Cannon is in the kitchen with me.

"You need any help?" he asks.

I'm so shaken by knowing he saw me that I drop one of the glasses on the kitchen floor.

"Oh my goodness, is everything okay?" Miss Wayne asks as he runs into the kitchen. "You okay, Sky?" he asks again as he checks my stiff body for any cuts. I can't respond at first because my eyes are still glued onto Cannon's.

"I'm okay," I say putting the other glass on the counter.

"Let me get the drinks. Go sit down, honey. I'll clean this mess. I should have stop being so lazy and got it my damn self. After all I am the hostess."

Miss Wayne reaches in the cabinet to get another glass and is about to pour the Coke in the one I smeared with pussy juice when Cannon snatches it from him.

"Don't use this. It's dirty," he interjects then puts it in the sink and walks out the kitchen.

"Okay," Miss Wayne responds and smiles. "Girl Cannon is so attentive, chile. You got you a good man there, Parade."

Miss Wayne turns around and looks at me because I'm still stuck.

"Are you okay, baby?" he asks.

238   *Black and Ugly*

"Uh...yeah...I'm okay," I answer.

"Well, go sit down now. I got this," he demands as he pushes me out the kitchen.

I want to run out the door but everybody will know something's up. I wonder if he's gonna tell Parade what I did. But then I remember I don't have any intention on befriending them after tonight anyway. So in a way, it doesn't even matter.

I casually walk to the sofa and act like nothing happened.

CHAPTER 33

MISS WAYNE

What I'd like to know is what's really going on with Miss Sky. She has been so distant lately and although I know her and Miss Parade have their problems, she's been taking it out on everyone else too. I hadn't seen her ever since we picked Miss Daffany up from the hospital. Well, I'm not gonna be too concerned with Ms. Thang anymore. I have decided that after tonight, if she continues to play her little games, I'm severing our friendship.

"How you feeling Miss Daffany?" I ask.

"I'm good. Just a little out of it that's all," she responds.

Poor chile hasn't been the same for a minute. And I have a feeling that I know what it is, it was probably my big mouth that brought things out. I think she's HIV positive. Damn! We're too young to be getting shit like that. But I don't care what she got she'll always be my girl and I'll always love her.

"Let's start the game," Miss Sky says, clearly not getting enough attention. "I think it was my turn to start first since Parade started first last month."

"Okay," everyone agrees.

"Well, Miss Wayne," she says as she turned around to me, "truth or dare?"

"Uhn-ahn, honey. We playing Charades this month, remember? We played that game last month and you know we have to switch up."

"*Noooooo*," Miss Sky asserts. "We didn't finish playing because Melvin came by and picked up Parade." She turns around and looks at Parade like she's sorry. "Oh, I'm sorry, Parade. I didn't mean to bring up your boyfriend," she pronounces real slyly.

"Don't worry, Sky. Melvin and me are through. And I told Cannon everything he needs to know about him," Miss Parade responds calmly.

"I doubt that very seriously," Miss Sky shoots back. We all look at one another trying to figure out what's up with her 'tude.

Right in the middle of the game, Miss Parade's cell phone rings. She excuses herself, walks out of the living room and goes into the bathroom to take the call. Miss Daffany jumps up heading to the kitchen.

Miss Parade returns five minutes later and she doesn't have her cell phone on her and that definitely doesn't help matters. As expected, Miss Sky has an attitude probably assuming it was Jay, while I wouldn't be surprised if it was. I figure she must've left the phone wherever on purpose but I almost ask,

By T. Styles   241

"Parade who was that?" until I reconsider. There's no need in me hot boxing. And after the little stunt Miss Sky pulled before by wanting to use her phone nobody really wants to hear her mouth.

"Sorry, ya'll. Uh...that was my mom," Miss Parade says.

"I bet it was," Miss Sky responds and rolls her eyes. "I don't recall you leaving to talk to your mom in the past. But, whatever you say...anyway," Miss Sky continues in her funky little demeanor, "Miss Wayne, truth or dare?"

"Truth," I say not wanting to act up as of yet by picking dare in front of Miss Parade's man.

"Okay. Is it true that you got that outfit for 10 bucks at the flea market in Baltimore?"

Oh this bitch tried it. See I wasn't gonna take it there but since she wants to bring it I decides to come for her when I get my turn.

"Yes, honey. It *is* true. Miss Wayne knows how to look for a deal without being cheap. Something you know a lot about," I retort and roll my neck.

"You look good in it too," Miss Daffany says as she returns from the kitchen looking like she's out to lunch. But I don't care. Whatever she took she deserves to feel better after everything she's been through.

"Thanks, baby. I try," I reply as I smack my lips and look back at Miss Sky as the trash she is. "My turn. Truth or dare, Miss Daffany?"

"True," Miss Daffany responds.

"Is it true that you seen Miss Sky eat a fry off the floor after it fell off her plate in Fridays?"

"It is true," Miss Daffany answers as she winks at me and everyone including Cannon busts out laughing.

"That is real cute but it was *my* food," Miss Sky responds.

"But it was on the fucking floor. Yuck," I tease as I brush her away to give Miss Daffany a high five. "And you call yourself a lady."

"Don't be mad, Sky. We just messing with you," Miss Parade says.

"Yeah, whatever the fuck," Miss Sky counters.

"*Okay*," says Miss Parade, thinking she's playing. But I know the bitch is serious.

"Truth or dare, Sky," Miss Daffany asks.

"*Truth*," she responds real nasty.

"Is it true you think that everyone in the world is jealous of you?" Miss Daffany laughs convincing me even more that she's high.

"It's true. Because they are jealous including all of you bitches in here."

"Hold up, Miss Sky. Are you playing or serious?" I ask her not feeling the attitude anymore.

"Why, Miss Wayne," she pauses, "I'm just playing. Just like ya'll are," she says sarcastically. "But since you asked me a question, truth or dare."

"Truth," I reluctantly respond as I try to think of what I could have possibly done around her that she could use against me. I stop as I realize that we've been friends so long it's a waste of my time.

"Is it true that you once thought Parade looked like a boy, and you didn't want to be her friend because she always looked dirty?"

"You bitch. You fucking bitch," I scream at her, wanting to slap her face.

What hurts the most is the look on Miss Parade's face as she waits for my answer.

"True or false?" Miss Sky repeats trying to make matters worse. "Why you keeping everybody waiting?"

"I heard you, bitch," I yell in her face. "It's true," I answer in a low voice. "But we were in fucking middle school then," I continue, trying to cover up the betrayal. "What…were we like 10?"

"Miss Wayne, we're not playing truth, dare and explanations so save it. If you said it you said it. This is a game right? We should all be able to handle anything we're dealt," she says and smiles at me.

244   *Black and Ugly*

I look over at Miss Parade who is visibly heartbroken and embarrassed and say, "I guess so."

CHAPTER 34

PARADE

I don't want to play the game anymore and I can tell that nobody besides Sky wants to play either. Sky embarrasses me so much that I want to go home and hide under my covers. Cannon's constant pulls around my waist make me feel better. I can tell he wants me to know that he's on my side and it feels good. But Sky has hurt my feelings for the last time.

"Truth or dare, Sky?" I ask. It's my turn.

"Truth," she responds like she's ready for me.

"Is it true that you never really liked me and only used me for what I could do for you?"

"False," she answers and laughs. "Are you kidding me? What can you do for me, Parade? You can't do shit for me but get in my way and try to bite my style. Bitch, I made you. Just a few weeks ago you were busted and look at you now."

"Now who's getting mad?" Miss Wayne says trying to help me as usual.

"I'm not mad. She asked me a question and I answered it. It's mothafucking false 'cuz never would I want you around me for anything you can do for me. You can't do shit for me. You ain't even got your own car. I think your tracks are too tight or something because you real funny tonight. You probably wearing a pair of my old panties right now."

"Stop, Sky," I yell at her as I begin to breathe hard and start crying.

"Stop what? It's true. You been biting my style for too fucking long trying to steal my man and shit behind my back."

"Your man left right in front of you," I remind her.

"Yeah, but you helped didn't you? Did you fuck him real good? It's okay, Parade. You might as well be honest now. He dumped me. He fucking dumped me tonight and it's all your fault."

"Sky, calm down. Why you always got to turn stuff into something about you?" Daffany asks.

"Yeah. You doing shows, Miss Sky," Miss Wayne adds.

"And what about you, Daffany? You have a fucking nerve. When you gonna tell everybody that you HIV positive instead of spreading that shit around? A whore with HIV, ain't that something?" she says as she shakes her head.

"What?" Daffany yells as she sits up. "It was you? You stole my papers?"

"I didn't steal your papers. I saw them lying on the floor and I grabbed them up thinking they were important and they were."

"So why didn't you tell me?"

"I forgot. And like I said, when the fuck are you gonna stop playing games and stop spreading that shit around?" Everyone is quiet and she continues, "All ya'll funny. Think just because I don't say nothing that I don't know shit." She stands. "Ya'll thought the joke was on me and ya'll were gonna make me embarrassed but I turned the shit around didn't I?"

Silence.

"And Cannon," she says as she looks at him, "stop playing with that girl's feelings because anybody as fine as you, don't want anything to do with Parade. Dump her right now while it's easy," she continues as she walks toward the door, "and don't worry I'll let myself out."

"Hold up for a second, Sky," Cannon interjects so calmly that his voice is like a knife cutting the tension in the air. "I haven't gotten my turn yet."

She turns around, looks at him and laughs. "What?" she says as if he's joking.

"I said I haven't gotten my turn yet."

"Oh, so what ya'll planned this?" she asks, looking around the room then sitting back down on the couch. "So what ya'll told him all my business and now he wanna play too? Okay," she continues as she wipes the tears from her face. "Shoot."

"Thanks," he adds real calmly. "Ask me, Parade. It's your turn so you have to ask me something."

I take a deep breath and try to focus on the game although I don't want to play. I'm also trying to figure out why he's doing this. Maybe he wants to calm everybody down and figures this is the best way to help.

"Is it true," I ask as I feel tears forming in my eyes, "that you think I'm attractive because I really need to know if you're playing games with me and I need to know right now. You heard about my faults and you know about all my secrets. You've met ugly Parade Knight who slept with her best friend's man because she admired her so much that she wanted to see what it was like to be like her. And I was wrong. I'm sorry, Sky," I continue as I turn to look at her. "I wish I could take it back but I can't. So, Cannon knowing all this, knowing who I really am I'd like to know - do you really think I'm attractive and do you really care about me because if you don't I can take it. You taught me a lot about myself and no matter what, I'm better now than I was before so, true or false, do you really care about me?"

He grabs my hands and says, "Parade, I came here on business of the worst kind. And at first I thought you were just another pretty face. With that being said, I'll answer the first part of your question by saying that no matter what happens I've always thought you were beautiful and not just because of how you look but because of who you are on the inside too. I love your eyes, your smile and the way you make me feel," he continues as Miss Wayne pushes me from behind while whispering, "I told you so."

"But, the best quality I love about you is your commitment to your friends and the people you care about. And I don't know what happened to make you do what you did to Sky but I can definitely say that if he left her she helped. She's the most selfish person I've met in my life." He looks at Sky, back at me then says "But I can feel the love in you and that's tight it's real. Maybe in another time and another life we can be together but not as boyfriend and girlfriend, as man and wife."

His response blows me away and I turn around to look at Miss Wayne and Daffany who are also crying. Sky holds her head low and doesn't face me.

I wipe the tears from my face and say, "Thank you, baby. That means so much to me. It's your turn."

He takes a deep breath and his entire expression changes as if he's becoming another person.

"Truth or dare, Sky?" he asks real coldly like he never said any of the nice things that just exited his mouth.

"Truth," she says shrugging like she doesn't want to play anymore.

"Is it true that you stabbed and murdered Melony Parker?"

CHAPTER 35

PARADE

"What's going on, Parade?" Sky asks. "Why he asking me that?" She cuts her eyes at me wondering if I sold her out.

"I don't know, Sky," I say real slowly, "but maybe you shouldn't say anything else." I look at him and back at her.

"No maybe she should," he says as he pulls out a gun and places it on his lap. "Baby, get on the couch with everybody else. I'm so sorry I gotta do this."

We all jump on Miss Wayne's pink couch, which can comfortably seat six people but because we are so scared we cram tightly together and hold one another closely.

"Now, I want everybody to calm down," he explains growing irritated by our whines and cries. "And if ya'll are cool only the person I'm looking for will get hurt."

His comment doesn't do anything but make matters worse. We may have had our problems but I think I can speak for everybody when I say nobody wants anybody to die.

Black and Ugly

"Why...uh...I don't understand this, Cannon," I ask as my cries join those of my friends. "I don't understand why you're doing this."

"I know it's real fucked up, baby," he says as he places the gun back in his lap with the barrel still facing our way, "but I'm a hit-man, paid to kill the person who murdered Melony Parker. I have my own ideas of who did it but I need to be sure. And that's where you ladies come in. Mr. Parker is very serious about taking care of whoever killed his wife so there are several other things we must talk about first. Number one, I'm going to kill somebody tonight. I need you all to understand that."

"Cannon, please don't do this," Miss Wayne yells.

Cannon just looks and silences him with his stare.

"Number two, the rest of you will be responsible for convincing me that you won't bring heat back on my client by running to the cops and opening your mouths and if I'm not convinced not *totally* convinced I'm putting a bullet in all four of your heads tonight."

Our cries and pleas for him not to kill us grow louder and Cannon is still visibly irritated but remains professional. All this does is make him appear even more insensitive and scarier.

"So you did lie to me? You lied to me about who you are."

"No I didn't. I told you I'm in the disposal business. So how did I lie?" he says as he looks at me, awaiting a response.

I don't have one. And even if I did I wouldn't say it because I'm too embarrassed and hurt by his ultimate plan. He did tell me he was in the disposal business and that he was responsible for removing trash but never in my wildest dreams did I think that meant killing one of us.

"I didn't lie and I meant everything I said to you. There's no reason for me to lie to you, Parade. I've had you already and right now...I'm the one holding the gun. Please believe me when I was hired I wasn't prepared for you and I wish you weren't involved in this shit. But don't think for one minute I won't kill you if you don't tell me what I need to know."

He then turns his attention back to Sky who I'm pretty sure knows it's coming. But what I don't understand is why or how he suspects her. Although I don't want to ask I want to know.

"Why do you think we have anything to do with it?" I inquire trying to cause a diversion.

"Good question," he responds as he smiles at me. "I understand that you ladies made a hell of an exit the night of the party. And I also understand this lady right here..." he points his gun at Sky, "had blood all over her pants that night so as far as I'm concerned she's either the one or she knows who did it."

"Please, Cannon you don't have to do this. Plus people saw you around us. If one of us ends up dead other people will know something," Daffany interrupts.

"What was the contingency of number two, Daffany?"

She shakes her head as if she forgot although I didn't.

He answers his question by saying, "You have to *convince* me that whoever remains will not bring heat back to my client. If I'm not *convinced* tonight that every one of you will remain silent I'm killing *all* of you."

"But why?" Daffany pleads.

"Because I can't worry about one of you convincing the others to go to the authorities when I get home. That's why it is imperative that you make me believe the survivors will remain quiet. Now you should know that I have a lot of information on you and your families. The cops that you've been working with report to me so you can already gather from your conversations with the fake officers how much I know. I even have your addresses."

"So the...cops...uh...weren't real?" I ask.

"I like to send them first to find out what's up before I even get off the plane. A lot of time they eliminate the legwork for me but since you all appear to be pretty loyal to one another I had to go deeper undercover. If they'd confirmed the killer I would've never met you, Parade. But I'm sure I would've seen you at one of your friends funerals." He smiles at me.

I hate him. And I hate how I allowed him into my heart only to hurt my friends and me. I can't believe he's the same man I shared my body with the same man who, just earlier in the day I made love to. He's the friendliest and most professional murderer I ever met but I'm terrified of him.

"Now for the last time I'm gonna go down the row and ask each of you one time and one time only who you believe murdered Melony and why. If you don't tell me what I need to know and I don't hear a yes by either the person who did it or the person who knows something I'll have to kill all of you."

My mind is working overtime, and I hope theirs are too. I don't want any of us to be hurt but unless one of us thinks of something quick I can't guarantee our safety. For some reason a plan pops in my head and if it goes the other way it can end up with all of us being killed. But right now it's our *only* alternative.

"Can I go to the bathroom?" I ask him as I stand.

"Why all of a sudden?" he questions sensing I'm on some bullshit.

"'Cuz I'm scared and my stomach is bubbling. I'll be quick please," I plead as I start moving up and down in place. "You owe me that, Cannon."

"Well hurry up," he says politely. "And Parade..."

"Yeah," I reply as I turn around before entering the bathroom.

"Don't fuck me."

"I won't," I respond and run in the bathroom.

Once inside I grab my cell phone I had stuffed in the hamper earlier. I put it there because I didn't want Sky asking me to use it again and seeing Jay's number. He called telling me he ended the relationship with her like that will make me want him again. Stuffing my phone in the hamper was dumb but it was all I could think of at the time. If she would've asked to use it I had plans to tell her I didn't know where it was. I guess it was a waste of my time considering she already knew about Jay and me anyway.

Quickly I look for the number and when I find it Cannon yells from the living room, "Parade, make it quick."

I wonder if his real name is even Cannon. I won't bother asking him though because I'm sure he wouldn't tell me.

"Okay," I yell back.

The pressure is killing me. I cut the water on to muffle the sound hit send and pray he will answer his phone.

"Markee, it's Parade."

"Awww shit. What up, yo?" he says.

"I was calling to see if you seen Miss Wayne. I just carried all these purses in his house and he ain't here."

"Oh…uh…naw, young. I ain't seen that nigga," he replies in a devious tone.

Suddenly Cannon knocks on the door and I can tell he's using the butt of his gun to do it. I muffle the sound on the phone from Markee and sit on the toilet as if Cannon can see me.

"Yes?" I respond as if I'm in pain.

"What you doing, baby?" he says in a creepy tone.

"I'm using the bathroom. I'll be right out."

"So why the water on?"

"'Cuz I can't concentrate without it," I utter praying that he bought it.

Silence.

"Hurry up. We got business to take care of out here."

"Okay."

"The next time I knock on the door, finished or not, I'm dragging you out by your hair."

"Okay."

He's gone so I turn my attention back to Markee.

Black and Ugly

"What you doing, yo? He there yet?"

"No," I say trying to sound disappointed. "I guess I have to leave all his shit in his house. Oh well I gotta go."

"I'm out," he states and gets off the phone really quickly.

I know immediately that my plan worked or at least I hope it did. Otherwise, why would he get off the phone so fast with me? Any other time he would be pressed to talk because he stayed asking me when I was gonna call him and shit. I know he has all intentions of busting in Miss Wayne's place to rob it. It's just a matter of time while time is exactly what we don't have a lot of right now.

I could've called the police but I didn't because I believe Cannon when he says that he'd have somebody to kill us. For all I know he'll hire another set of fake cops to take us out. But this way, Markee can bust in and at least cause a diversion long enough for us to help Sky out.

I walk out of the bathroom and make sure Miss Wayne's bedroom door is open. I walk in the living room and sit down. Everybody is still shaken up and Daffany quickly wraps her arms around me.

"You finish?" Cannon asks like he knows I'm up to something.

"Yes."

"Good. I'm gonna start with Wayne first," he says.

"Miss Wayne," I interject.

"What?" he asks.

"I said he likes to be called Miss Wayne," I answer using the silliest things to buy time.

"Sweetheart, I appreciate your help but this gentleman has a gun. So at this time he can call me anything he wants," Miss Wayne adds.

"Thank you cuz but I'm not into calling another man Miss anything so...Wayne, did you or do you have any idea who killed Melony Parker that night?" he asks real slowly.

I hope that Markee is rounding everybody up and not wasting time. I've never looked forward to a robbery in all my life.

"Cannon," I say, trying to cause another diversion.

"Yes," he responds as if he's extra irritated with me.

"Are you gonna give us enough time to answer the question first? Like five minutes or so."

"Naw," he says, looking at me. "We don't have that much time. And don't interrupt me again, Parade. This is not a fucking game. Answer the question, Wayne."

"No," he says as he shakes his head. "I don't know who killed that woman and I'm so sorry I don't. Can you tell Mr. Parker I said that I'm so sorry about what happened to his wife?"

"Yes but do you have an idea of who may have done it?"

Again he shakes his head no.

"Wayne, I need you to answer the question."

"No...uh...no I don't," Miss Wayne articulates as he begins to cry.

"Daffany."

"Yes," she says, crying as hard as everybody else.

"Yes, you do know?" he asks thinking she's telling him something.

"No, I don't," she responds and puts her head down. "But I wish I did. I'm so sorry."

He then moves to me looking into my eyes as if he knows I know something. Sky grabs my arm and squeezes it tightly and I can tell she's worried that I will betray her.

"Parade, baby do you know who killed Melony?"

"No. I don't know anything," I answer quickly and prepare to give my life for the only true family I ever had. If I have to die beside them I'm going to. And I know they feel the same otherwise they would have given up Sky too because although they don't know for sure I know they suspect her.

"Well you know what this means. If Sky doesn't admit to killing her or denies killing her I'll have to tell my chop men to get four body bags. So, Sky did you kill Melony Parker that night?"

"Yes," she says as she busts out crying. "Yes I did but please don't hurt my friends."

Up until this moment we all thought Sky was selfish and only cared about herself but here she is admitting to the ultimate crime in order to save our lives.

"I knew you did but to be honest I thought you'd sell your friends out."

"Uh…how…uh…did you know?" Sky cries.

"Because you're wearing her one-of-a-kind canary yellow diamond pendant necklace. I needed to get a good look at it and since it's dim in the living room I followed you in the kitchen."

"Well," he says as he stands and grabs a pillow. "Lay down on the floor."

"Oh God no! Please don't. Please don't kill her," we all scream.

"Shut the fuck up," he yells as he points the gun at us and silences all the crying, "or I'll kill you mothafuckas anyway."

Sky reluctantly gets face down on the floor crying. He places the pillow to the back of her head cocks the gun and before he pulls the trigger someone is rattling the door.

"Shut the fuck up," Cannon whispers harshly but loud enough for us to hear. "You expecting somebody, mothafucka?" he asks Miss Wayne.

"No." He shakes his head rapidly. And before he could say anything else we hear them prying at the door.

"Everybody get on the floor," Cannon commands as he grabs us by our arms and cuts off the light.

The door creeps open and in the dark I push my friends toward Miss Wayne's bedroom. The sounds of several footsteps let me know Markee bought more than one person. Unnoticed we're able to get into Miss Wayne's bedroom and lock the door.

"Who the fuck is that?" a voice yells.

"Who the fuck are you?" Cannon hollers back.

"Don't worry 'bout it, mothafucka."

"You came at the wrong time, man. You better get the fuck out of here," Cannon shouts.

"Fuck you, nigga. We ain't going a mothafucking place and you ain't either so what you try to beat us to the purses?" Markee asks.

"Purses? What the fuck are you talking about? What are you some type of gay bandit?" Cannon questions.

"You calling me gay?" Markee asks. "Fuck this shit. You calling me gay, mothafucka?"

"Markee...is that you, man?" Cannon inquires.

Now I'm worried. I didn't know they knew each other. Damn! I'm sure they're gonna work together to kill all of us anyway. My little plan backfired and it's all my fault. My stomach is churning knots and I feel like I can throw up.

"Yeah," he responds apparently recognizing him too.

"What you doing here, man? You fucking shit up."

"Shit! My fucking brother's gonna kill me. Shit! Shit! I didn't know you were in here, man. Parade called me and told me some purses were here and I was trying to jack them joints before the faggy came home."

"Okay...just walk out and let me handle my business. I'll never tell your brother you were here," Cannon says real smoothly.

"Sorry, yo I can't do that."

BANG, BANG, BANG.

We all hold one another and start crying as we hear the sound of a body dropping to the floor. We all want resolution but hearing the shots scare us even more. Someone immediately approaches the door and we know it's Markee.

"Who in there? Open this fucking door. Parade, I know you set me up, bitch. I'ma kill your ass. Don't think that just because I killed this nigga that hit on ya'll's head ain't going through. You ain't buy nothing but a few more seconds."

"Oh my God. I'm so sorry, ya'll. I made things worse," I tell them.

"I love ya'll," Daffany says, feeling like the rest of us - that things are all over now and that we are certainly going to die. We know that if he fills the tiny room with bullets we'll all be dead. There is nowhere to escape not even in the closet because it sits directly opposite the bedroom door.

We continue to say our good-byes get on the floor and hold one another as we hear the shots ring out. They stop and we feel our bodies.

"What...uh...happened?" I ask as if they know.

"I don't know," Daffany says as she lets me go.

"I think we okay," Sky adds.

"Oh. I forgot. That's a metal door." Miss Wayne laughs.

He says that and I drop to my knees and thank God. We all knew his door is metal but in all the commotion forgot.

"FREEZE. THIS IS THE POLICE!"

Hearing those words for once in our lives are like music to our ears. We stay in the room while listening to the suspect being hauled off. Next we hear authoritative knocks on the metal door.

"Is anybody in there?" an officer yells.

"Yes!" we say simultaneously.

"Please open this door!" the voice repeats.

I think about Cannon hiring fake cops and say, "With all due respect, can you slide your badge under the door? We've been having run-ins with fake cops lately." We all bust out laughing.

"No problem, ma'am," he answers as he slides his badge under the door.

EPILOGUE

SIX MONTHS LATER

PARADE

Life is different. I moved away from the Manor because I couldn't stay around there anymore. Everything about that place reminds me of a life I hate and gives me bad feelings.

The night everything jumped off we were all worried that something bad would eventually happen to us but with Markee shooting Cannon three times in the chest we felt positive that we would be okay. We were wrong because the next day Sky was murdered.

It was terrible. Whoever killed her did a far worse job than what Cannon would have done. They stabbed her so many times in the face that she was unrecognizable and because her parents were both witnesses they did the same to them. It was a closed-casket funeral and we were so scared that none of us went. Later an anonymous call came to my phone threatening to handle us if we opened our mouths. Needless to say we didn't.

Daffany admitted to having HIV and went to the doctor to get meds. She claims that she's stop having sex for money but Miss Wayne says he still sees her hanging out with certain men around the neighborhood. I just hope she's safe. We hang out sometimes but only if she comes to my place over here in Riverdale Maryland, which is about 20 minutes away.

Miss Wayne moved, too with a man he met on Myspace.com. They've been doing pretty good and he visits around the way more than I do. He says he has to because his family and everything he ever knew, is still there. Unlike him I don't have shit to say to my mother or a reason to go back so if it wasn't for him I'd never know what was going on.

Miss Wayne is somebody I'll never stop talking to because he's the one person I truly consider family. I'm happy for him and his new friend and hope it lasts because I hear gay male relationships usually don't. They live in Largo Maryland, which is an upscale part of the state about 45 minutes from me. Whenever I talk to him he tells me he's getting dicked down with 11-inches or something else nasty like that. He's such a freak. Just as long as he's happy I'm good.

Markee was convicted for the murder of Russell Hargrove aka Eclipse aka Cannon. But he didn't last three days in jail because Jay paid somebody to sodomize him with a broom handle and slit his throat. He said it was for raping his niece and stealing her

ATM card, a couple of months back. They found out he was responsible for that, too, after running his prints. I guess all the shit he did finally caught up with his ass, literally. So Silver and Jay have major beef now.

Anyway, I'm on my way to meet Daffany and Miss Wayne at PG Plaza. I can't wait to see them because I miss them so much. That's one thing I can say is different about where I live now. Back at the Manor I had all my friends accessible. Now I don't. When they arrive at the mall we all hug for five minutes as if we didn't just see each other last week.

"Hey, girl," Miss Wayne screams. "I'm loving your hair. You done got all fly on a nigga and shit. DO IT BITCH YEOOUUUSSSSS!" he says as he hit my arm.

"Thank you, baby. Working at that salon pays off. I get my hair done free because they don't like their employees looking any kind of way," I tell him.

What's sad is that since everything happened with Sky and I left home I finally started feeling better about myself. Maybe I should've distanced myself from certain people who brought me down a long time ago. Now I realize that I'm black and beautiful. It's a shame it took a murderer to show me that. But I'm still hiding a secret from my friends. And that is, I have a new man and it's serious. The only thing is he's a drug dealer too. I met him a week after Sky's murder.

In the wake of Daffany's HIV status I decided to go get tested. I went to the clinic in downtown D.C. that gives immediate results. I had unprotected sex with too many men including Melvin and Jay. I'm sure Sky was having unprotected sex with Jay too and who knows if either of them was fucking Daffany so I was scared. Thank God I'm negative. After receiving my results I decided to go to Arundel Mills Mall and buy a new pair of shoes. A diamond necklace in the window of a jewelry store caught my eye as I was leaving the mall. I stopped to look and stood there staring at it for few minutes. I searched through my purse already knowing I didn't have enough cash to make the purchase. I couldn't help but think about Cannon and everything he did for me when I thought he was real. I'm sure he would have bought the necklace for me in another time and in another life...just as a tear fell down my cheek I felt a tap on my shoulder. I turned around.

"Excuse me, I just wanted to tell you that you are absolutely beautiful," he said. "I mean stunning."

"Thank you," I responded and smiled as I wiped my tear. *Damn! He's fine.* I thought and continued to smile. He has smooth deep chocolate skin with strong facial features. I bet you Sky would not have called him black and ugly even though he was dark. His complexion matched mines to a "T" and in a way I felt connected to him because of it. He was handsome flawless and clean from head to toe. At that point I understood what Miss Wayne was talking about when referring to them chocolate boys. His eyes were bright and round with thick lashes topped with perfect brows while his lips are full and extremely kissable. "You're very handsome yourself."

"Thank you," he replied. "I can't believe it...you remind me so much of my wife," his voice faded as he spoke those last few words. "What's your name?"

"Parade," I answered.

"*Parade?*" he responds. He looked surprised. His eyes roamed over my body. He appeared to be studying me. As I was about to ask him if he knew me a woman approached with a crying baby.

"Excuse me," he said as he took the baby from her and held him in his arms. He continued to study me. "He misses his mother." I raised my left eyebrow. "She passed..." I felt bad for him because the baby eased up a little but continued to whine. For some reason, the little boy looked at me and paused. I sat my bag and my purse on the floor then reached my arms out and he came to me. I rocked him a bit then rubbed his back and he smiled at his daddy. He tried to pull at my hair but I caught the grip of his palm rattled his soft little hand then ran it across the side of my face. He laughed.

"And your name is?" I asked since I was holding his baby.

"Carvelas, but everybody calls me Smokes," he said. It looked like a light bulb went off in his head. "Have we met?" he questioned.

"No...I don't think so," I responded as I continued to make smiley faces at his child. "Do you know me?"

"Naw," he said clearing his throat. "I thought you were somebody else."

"Oh," I replied not knowing what else to say.

"Parade would you allow me to purchase that necklace for you?"

"Uh...what necklace?" I responded pretending not to know what he was referring to.

"The one I saw you looking at before I walked up on you. I mean, you were staring at it wasn't you?"

"Yeah," I said holding my head down. "It's beautiful."

"No...it's classy," he corrected me. "You're *beautiful*. I would really love for you to have it," he continued. "Just a small token of my appreciation."

"Appreciation for what?" I questioned wondering what I did to deserve such an expensive gift from a complete stranger. "I don't even know you."

"Trust me I know more about you than you think." His eyes were serious and almost scary but I trusted him.

"Why you say that?"

"I can just tell what kind of person you are," he responded.

"In that case," I smiled still holding the baby firmly in my arms. "Sure."

For once in my life I decided to let a man do what he wanted to for me. It wasn't like the situation with Jay and me. I wasn't being paid for a service.

When he disappeared into the store, I sat on a bench and the woman who was caring for the baby grabbed my bags and joined me. I was sure he was gonna say he left his money and couldn't buy it. Still I played with the child who liked the way I bounced him in my lap, until Smokes returned. He stepped behind me and I noticed his hairy arm as he placed the pendent around my neck. *Damn, He smells like money,* I thought. Then, I felt a tingling sensation take over my body. He placed a gentle kiss on my cheek and said, "This is just the beginning."

Since then we've been inseparable. That's why I had to keep brushing Jay off. Although he said he wanted to be with me after Sky was murdered I knew he could never be true to me. I guess he's the one with hurt feelings now.

I love spending time with Smokes. He makes me feel good to be me all over. Last night we were lying in my bed watching America's Next Top Model and he dug into a part of me that no man had ever explored before.

"Parade," he said, "as a child, what was the one thing you wanted out of life?"

"I don't know," I said shrugging my shoulders.

"Come on, baby," he persisted. "There has to be something."

"Well...I always wanted a family of my own," I told him without thinking. "I wanted to give a child the love that my mother never gave me."

"I wanna give you that and more, baby." He reached under the pillow, removed a little blue velvet box and opened it exposing the biggest diamond ring I had ever seen. "Parade, will you marry me," he asked.

I stared at it for a minute. I couldn't answer him right away. Nothing about the "now" seemed real to me. Where did he come from? One look at his home let me know he could have anybody he wanted. And here he was, asking me to be his wife.

"Yes, Smokes," I finally cried. "Yes I will be your wife."

He took my hand, slipped the ring on the appropriate finger and then kissed me passionately.

"I wish my friends could be here to share this moment with me," I responded.

"They will be," he whispered as he kissed me on the neck.

"Well...not all of them. Sky won't."

The look on his face went from love to anger.

"Listen," he said slowly. "From what you've told me about her she would've never been happy for you. Jealousy doesn't go away...it just grows."

"I know," I said looking at the comforter on our bed. "But she was my-"

"She was nothing to you!" he said raising his voice. I jumped and he continued only after reducing his tone. "I'm sorry for yelling but I hate hearing you talk about her like she was down for you. The world is better off without that chick. My wife was taken by somebody just as scandalous as her. But you know what, I believe my wife sent you to me because we're good for each other. And everything...I mean everything happens for a reason. Including Sky's death."

"Why don't you have any pictures of her around here?" I dared to ask.

"I told you...it's too hard for me to look at them right now. Plus we're gonna make our own memories. But first you have to let the past go starting with Sky."

After that conversation I never brought up her name again. For some reason I could tell she was a touchy subject for him. What I didn't know was why. A few days later he asked me to pick out an outfit so that he could introduce me to his family at his home in Virginia. He wants me to look my absolute best as he introduces me to his parents. That's how I ended up at the mall with Miss Wayne and Daffany.

"Daffany, so what's up, girl?" I say as I tap her shoulder while we are walking toward the food court.

"Nothing. Just doing me." She smiles which probably means she's doing the same thing. As long as she looks good and is taking her meds I'm happy for her. Who am I to judge?

"So are we gonna shop or what? I ain't come here to stare you bitches in the face all day," Miss Wayne yells. "I need some new damn shoes."

"You got that right," I tell him as I reach in my Coach bag and pull out the stack of cash my fiancé gave me earlier.

"Um...I wonder where you got *that* from," he says, "and that..." He continued pointing to my ring.

Before he can finish and I can say anything a sighting scares the hell out of us. There in the mall stands the girl who as far as we know is supposed to be dead. It's the same girl that, for the longest, Sky kept blaming me for her death. And it's the exact same girl I beat down in the mall.

Me, Miss Wayne and Daffany just stare at her as she looks at us like she's hoping we don't bother her. But, I have to say something. I need an answer. I walk over to her politely as she jumps the moment I step.

"Excuse me. I'm so sorry for what happened a while back and I'm not going to hurt you but I do need to know something."

The girl throws her hand up and says, "Look I don't have time for this shit," and begins to walk away.

"This will be really quick," I continue approaching her. "I'm not trying to start anything. I just need to know if you ever heard of a Melony Parker?" I ask since I think it's her name. It quickly, becomes obvious that she's certainly not the girl that Sky led me to believe died at Donna's party. *So, who was Melony?*

"No but I know of her," she says politely. Miss Wayne and Daffany draw closer to hear her response. "She was that drug dealer's wife wasn't she? The one that got killed. I think his name is Smokes."

"Smokes?" I respond and touch my necklace. The room began to spin but I remained calm. "Thank you," I say somehow maintaining my composure."

"No problem," she smiles. "I almost didn't recognize you until I saw your eyes. You're very pretty when you ain't beating people up."

"Thanks," I smile back even though I feel that if somebody touches me I'd fall right over.

"Well…take care."

It all makes sense. Every picture of Smoke's wife was removed. There was nothing remaining that she ever existed in their home. Was that all for me? Did he want me that much that he'd erase the mother of his child's existence?

As I think about my problem Daffany explains to us that we've all seen him around the way. I promised her that I didn't because I stayed up under Melvin and Jay so much. Of course Daffany and Miss Wayne would know him because they lived in the streets. I lived in the house. She says that he drives a 2006 silver Mercedes Benz CLS55 with charcoal interior. It was the same car I drove to the mall today in. None of us made the connection because they used his government name on the news and never showed Melony's picture. Who would've known that Smokes and Mr. Parker were one in the same? I feel so stupid for not making the connection. It was easy to miss because the last name Parker is common.

I just assumed she was the girl from the mall because that's what Sky told me. At the same time I remain lost as to why Sky had beef with her until Miss Wayne put it in perspective by saying although Sky wore a lot of red her favorite color was green and that she probably wanted Melony's man. Once again Sky lied and it almost followed her to her grave. Almost.

Some how I got my shopping complete and say my goodbyes to my friends. As I leave the mall I don't dwell too long on discovering how my soul mate had my *best friend* killed for killing his wife. Did he make the call? But, after what I had been through on behalf of Sky I decided to let it go. I didn't want to see her dead but she had said enough for the both of us. I decided the past was the past and there's nothing I could do about it. Eventually I would tell Miss Wayne and Daffany that I'm going to marry the infamous Smokes, the one who killed one of our best friends. But...I knew now would not be a good time. Now that it's all said and done I feel like she hid more from me than I'll ever realize. It's obvious she only used me to protect her since she couldn't protect herself. But like my fiancé says everything happens for a reason and life goes on...and my life begins right now...with him...as Mrs. Parade Parker.

The Cartel Publications Order Form

www.thecartelpublications.com

Inmates **ONLY** receive novels for $10.00 per book.

(Mail Order **MUST** come from inmate directly to receive discount)

Shyt List 1	_____	$15.00
Shyt List 2	_____	$15.00
Shyt List 3	_____	$15.00
Shyt List 4	_____	$15.00
Shyt List 5	_____	$15.00
Pitbulls In A Skirt	_____	$15.00
Pitbulls In A Skirt 2	_____	$15.00
Pitbulls In A Skirt 3	_____	$15.00
Pitbulls In A Skirt 4	_____	$15.00
Victoria's Secret	_____	$15.00
Poison 1	_____	$15.00
Poison 2	_____	$15.00
Hell Razor Honeys	_____	$15.00
Hell Razor Honeys 2	_____	$15.00
A Hustler's Son 2	_____	$15.00
Black and Ugly	_____	$15.00
Black and Ugly As Ever	_____	$15.00
Year Of The Crackmom	_____	$15.00
Deadheads	_____	$15.00

Black and Ugly

The Face That Launched A

Thousand Bullets _____ $15.00

The Unusual Suspects _____ $15.00

Miss Wayne & The Queens of DC _____ $15.00

Paid In Blood (eBook Only) _____ $15.00

Raunchy _____ $15.00

Raunchy 2 _____ $15.00

Raunchy 3 _____ $15.00

Mad Maxxx _____ $15.00

Quita's Dayscare Center _____ $15.00

Quita's Dayscare Center 2 _____ $15.00

Pretty Kings _____ $15.00

Pretty Kings 2 _____ $15.00

Pretty Kings 3 _____ $15.00

Silence Of The Nine _____ $15.00

Silence Of The Nine 2 _____ $15.00

Prison Throne _____ $15.00

Drunk & Hot Girls _____ $15.00

Hersband Material _____ $15.00

The End: How To Write A _____ $15.00

Bestselling Novel In 30 Days (Non-Fiction Guide)

Upscale Kittens _____ $15.00

Wake & Bake Boys _____ $15.00

Young & Dumb _____ $15.00

Young & Dumb 2: _____ $15.00

Tranny 911 _____ $15.00

By T. Styles

Tranny 911: Dixie's Rise _____ $15.00

First Comes Love, Then Comes Murder _____ $15.00

Luxury Tax _____ $15.00

The Lying King _____ $15.00

Crazy Kind Of Love _____ $15.00

And They Call Me God_____ $15.00

The Ungrateful Bastards _____$15.00

Lipstick Dom _____ $15.00

A School of Dolls _____ $15.00

KALI: Raunchy Relived _____ $15.00

Please add $4.00 **PER BOOK** for shipping and handling.

The Cartel Publications * P.O. BOX 486 OWINGS MILLS MD 21117

Name: _____

Address: _____

City/State: _____

Contact# & Email:

_____

Please allow 5-7 <u>BUSINESS</u> days <u>Before</u> shipping.

The Cartel Publications is <u>NOT</u> responsible for prison orders rejected.

<u>NO PERSONAL CHECKS ACCEPTED</u>

<u>STAMPS NO LONGER ACCEPTED</u>

Black and Ugly

CPSIA information can be obtained
at www.ICGtesting.com
Printed in the USA
LVHW020506101118
596627LV00001B/26/P